FEMME

FEMME

METTE BACH

James Lorimer & Company Ltd., Publishers
Toronto

James Lorimer & Company Ltd., Publishers acknowledges the support of the Ontario Arts Council. We acknowledge the financial support of the Government of Canada through the Canada Book Fund for our publishing activities. We acknowledge the support of the Canada Council for the Arts which last year invested $24.3 million in writing and publishing throughout Canada. We acknowledge the Government of Ontario through the Ontario Media Development Corporation's Ontario Book Initiative.

  Canadä

Cover image: Shutterstock

Library and Archives Canada Cataloguing in Publication

Bach, Mette, 1976-, author
    Femme / Mette Bach.

Issued in print and electronic formats.
ISBN 978-1-4594-0768-8 (bound).--ISBN 978-1-4594-0767-1
(pbk.).--
ISBN 978-1-4594-0769-5 (epub)

    I. Title.

PS8603.A298F44 2015   jC813'.6   C2014-907517-0
C2014-907518-9

James Lorimer & Company Ltd.,   Distributed in the United States by:
Publishers   Orca Book Publishers
317 Adelaide Street West, Suite 1002 P.O. Box 468
Toronto, ON, Canada   Custer, WA USA
M5V 1P9   98240-0468
www.lorimer.ca

Printed and bound in Canada
Manufactured by Marquis in Montmagny, Quebec in February 2015.
Job # 111638

To Janine Fuller, Bruce Smyth, and the late Jim Deva of Little Sister's Bookstore & Art Emporium, for their commitment to intellectual freedom and books.

1

MAGICAL ANIMALS

The hall is crowded, so I barely notice Luanne Chen coming straight for me. She waves. I blow a kiss at her. We were inseparable in grades eight to eleven but ever since I started going out with Paul last year, I haven't had much time for her. I haven't been to Knitting Club or Interfaith in forever, even though I was the one who signed up both of us in the first place. So far this year, I've been too busy with my hot boyfriend and his crew. Who knew it was so much extra work moving up the popularity ladder?

The bell rings. Time for Slow Science.

Since I failed regular Biology 11 last year, I'm in a special class. We get to sit on our desks if we want, as long as we don't bring iPods or text our friends or fall asleep.

It's my turn to present to the class. I clip the pathetic poster I made last night to the top of the blackboard and take a deep breath.

"The kiwi bird is a magical animal. It doesn't have wings, so it can't fly and it's practically blind. New Zealand loves the bird anyway and named it their national bird."

If that's not an inspiring story, I don't know what is. A couple of people nod as if they get what I mean. Others yawn or stare out the window. I'm ready to sit down again, but Mr. Stetic says, "Magical is not exactly a scientific word, Sofie. Do you really believe the kiwi bird has magical powers?"

The class laughs. I want to die.

Mr. Stetic waits for my answer, but I stare at my turquoise Converse sneakers until he asks a different question.

"Can you tell us about the kiwi bird's

habitat, diet, and life expectancy?"

Beet red, I read the facts on the poster aloud. Later, I burn out of Slow Science five minutes early, even though Mr. Stetic's talking about homework. It's nearly impossible to fail this class, no matter what you do.

At my locker, I examine my eyeliner in the magnetic mirror and dab on some lip gloss. Just after the bell rings, I feel a familiar kiss on my neck and Paul's arms come around my middle to give me a squeeze.

"Hey, babe," he says. "How about hitting Semiahmoo Mall with me?"

"I have to talk to Mr. Davidson about English," I tell him, pouting.

"Blow him off. It's after three. It's sunny and I've got some good news."

"What is it?"

"I'm only telling you if you come for a snack."

He's such a flirt. It's impossible to say no to Paul's gorgeous smile.

"Alright." I turn and kiss him. He pulls me

in and kisses me deeply, right in the middle of the crowded hallway. Someone yells, "Get a room!" I turn and look, but I can't tell who said it.

Moments later, we're walking hand-in-hand toward the parking lot. Leaving school is the best part of the day, except for one tiny thing. Every afternoon, I have to search for my tin can in a parking lot filled with BMWs, Mercedes, and Volkswagens.

It's universally cool to have your own car when you're in high school and I am grateful, but mine comes with a catch: two huge yellow stickers advertising the family business, Sunny Side Cleaning. It's about as subtle as those Google Maps recorder-mobiles. It could have been worse. Mom actually wanted to add our photos. She's insane. I told her if we did that, the pictures would get defaced for sure. If not by hooligans, I'd do it myself. Unibrow for me. Hitler-stache for Mom. I mean, come on. Today I'm tucked in between Rachel Mackenzie, the prettiest girl in school, who drives her mom's Jeep, and Brooke-Lynn Bradley, the girl who starred in diaper commercials as a baby and now drives a Range Rover. She also happens to be Paul's ex.

I unlock the passenger side of my tin-can car for Paul. As he gets in, Slow Science and needing to talk with Mr. Davidson about English fade into memories.

We're eating at the food court, sitting beside each other at a table for four. "Are you ever going to tell me your big news?" I ask.

He puts his arm around me. "The big news is — " He stops chewing for a second, kisses me, and then says, "I love you."

"How's that news?"

His devilish smile appears. Those dimples.

I shake my head at him. When my burger is finished, I crumple up the paper and get up to toss it into the garbage. I look toward the exit, wondering if I should drive back to school. Maybe it's not too late to catch Mr. Davidson.

"Wait up," Paul says, grabbing onto my arm and walking behind me like he's a bad dog on a leash. I tell him about heading back to school.

"Since when do you care so much about English class?"

"Since I got partnered with Clea Thompson for the entire year. I don't think he understands what a huge mistake it is."

"Why?"

"Because I'm a C student, that's why. And Clea's some kind of genius. We're going to be graded together for a portion of our mark and she already told me she wants to get a scholarship."

Paul shrugs. "Don't worry about it."

"What do you mean, don't worry? I could single-handedly destroy her future." I can't believe he's being so chill about it.

"You got yourself a sweet deal. She can do all the work, while you sit back and enjoy the ride." He tries to high-five me, but I don't go for it.

"That's ridiculous and you know it. How can I face her week after week if I do that?

Huh?" I'm huffing now. An elderly woman on the bench beside us looks up from her crossword. I lower my voice. "I have to tell Mr. Davidson that I can't take part in this stupid new program. No way."

Paul puts his arms around me. "Hey now. I was just trying to cheer you up."

I manage to curl the sides of my mouth upward, but I'm not really smiling and he can tell.

"Don't worry, Sofie. No matter what happens, you have me. I'll take care of you."

I hate to admit it, but Paul's devotion feels like a consolation prize. I should be grateful that I have him — the prize of the school, charmer of parents and (amazingly) teachers, captain of the soccer team, the guy all the girls swarm.

"I don't want to be taken care of."

He takes my hand and draws it up to his mouth. It's a sweet movie moment that is supposed to sweep me off my feet like I'm Rachel McAdams and he's Ryan Gosling. But we're standing in front of a shoe outlet store and I'm watching a kid pick gum off the ground and eat it and I'm completely unable to be romanced. There are probably at least fifty girls who would love to trade places with me, bad grades and all, just to be here with Paul. He's not just good looking, with his dark features and soft, touchable boy-band hair, he's also really sweet. Infuriatingly so. He kisses the back of my hand while looking into my eyes.

Anyone would love Paul. Why doesn't it seem like enough?

He continues. "In June Uncle Gary is taking me on full-time at the dealership. Our lives are just beginning. You'll see."

I know he's trying to make me feel better, so I kiss him and tell him I love him. When I drop him off at his house a few minutes later, I tell him I love him again. I've been saying it a lot lately. Maybe I'm trying to convince myself that everything's perfect. You know the old saying, "Be careful what you wish for"? I used to pray to God to clear up my skin, make me popular enough that nobody bugs me, and give me the best boyfriend in the school. Now that I have all that, I should be happy, but I'm not. It's weird.

2

CURSED

It's Tuesday, so I'm making dinner. Mom and I take turns. She's got Saturdays, Mondays, and Wednesdays. I'm Sundays, Tuesdays, and Thursdays. On Friday nights, we order sushi or Thai. I hit the Save-on-Foods on my way home for salmon, asparagus, salad, and pie crusts. We have a lot of eggs at home, so I'm making quiche. Mom will be mildly annoyed that I'm over budget, but she'll be pleased that I made her favourite. Plus, there'll be enough left over for our lunches tomorrow.

I get to work in the kitchen, chopping onions and slicing mushrooms. Cooking takes my mind off the mood I've been in, at least for a little while. I stick my iPod in my back pocket, pop in my earbuds, and listen to the playlist Paul made for me. He has great taste in music.

Before I know it, my mom comes through the door.

"Honey, I'm home," she says in her joking, 1950s-sitcom way. "Oh, smells great in here."

I smile. "Ready to eat in fifteen?"

"I can be," she says. "Let me put these rags in the wash." She's lugging a blue IKEA bag filled with old, cut up T-shirts and towels that she uses for work. Tuesday is a big day for her. She cleans two of the huge houses near my school.

Clad in her yoga pants with her hair in pigtails, she pours herself a glass of red wine from a carton and comes to the table. She looks like an aerobics instructor. It's no wonder people don't think we're related. I look like her schlumpy sidekick in my shabby-chic vintage finds, my blue (or green or black) nails, and the ever-changing wonder that is my hair. Right now it's blue, but I'm going red on the weekend. I know Mom's not exactly into it, but she hasn't said anything.

"What's on the menu?"

"Salad, asparagus, and salmon quiche," I tell her.

"Oh," she says, "what have I done to deserve this?"

I take the quiche out of the oven and set it on the trivet between our two placemats. Then I grab the buttery asparagus. She's already digging into the greens. I sit.

"How was school?" she asks.

"Worst day ever," I say.

She raises an eyebrow and takes a sip of wine.

"Yeah. I got partnered up with this totally straight-A student who's like a prodigy or something, so I have to do better in English or I'll ruin her life."

"Well, then get studying. What are you waiting for?"

"Nothing." I feel like an idiot. Everything seems so simple when my mom talks about it. *Need to do better in school? Study!*

I wish life were as easy as she makes it seem. We eat in silence for a while.

"You know, when I was your age, I was terrible in school. I couldn't sit still, couldn't pay attention to my teachers."

"Really?"

"Maybe you're cursed with the same condition."

Cursed. I think about that. She takes another sip of wine. I don't say anything because I can tell she has more to say.

"As long as you work with it, you're okay. Look at me. Remember a few years back when I was laid off and we had nothing? I built this business from scratch. It was a lot of hard work, but I did it."

She takes another bite of quiche before saying, "If you're not good at school, be good at life."

"I know." I've heard her philosophy many times.

"What's new with Paul?" she asks through a mouthful of salad.

"He told me today that he wants to take care of me."

Mom scoffs. "Worst plan I've heard so far. Your father said the same thing. Look what happened."

My mom's always finding ways to put down Dad after their divorce. He moved back to Germany years ago and ever since then she's blamed him for abandoning me, even though she's the one who kicked him out.

Upstairs on my bed, I stare at the ceiling with my earbuds in again. I'm not doing anything. Sometimes, I think I really am lazy and destined to ruin my own life — as well as Clea Thompson's. But I know it's not true. I just haven't found anything I'm passionate about yet.

I doze off and when I wake up, it's past ten and I'm still in my school clothes. Mom's bedroom light is faint under her door, which means she's either reading a romance or saying her prayers before going to sleep. We only started going to church a few years back but she really takes it seriously. At first, she joked that it was a good place to meet men, but then she dated a few and the jokes stopped. Now she prays. She says it helps clear her mind and that it's the key to doing well in business. Personally, I think her business does well because we live in a neighbourhood full of old people and rich people. Around here, people either can't or won't do their own cleaning.

I change into one of Paul's old T-shirts. As I brush my teeth, I remember Mr. Davidson's exact words. This new program is mandatory and there are no exceptions. I guess it's pointless to resist. I'm sure Clea has already tried.

Back in my room, I wake up my sleeping computer. There's an e-mail from Clea. I sit there and stare at her name in my inbox for a while, not yet ready to open it and commit to piles of work. I'd give anything to have a bright future ahead of me, like she has in front of her — green lights in all directions. I read her brief message and then write back, asking her to come over tomorrow after school. Then I look around my room at all the clothes on the floor and the shelves of hair products, creams, soaps, perfumes, and makeup, as well as pictures of my grandparents and of Paul. Mom says my messiness is part of the problem. If that's true, I'm doomed.

I can't sleep, so I end up playing Candy Crush long into the night. Paul put it on my phone and now I'm obsessed. I finally nod off around three, with visions of striped, shiny candies dancing in front of me.

3

PROOF

Before school, there's another e-mail from Clea. It says she'd love to come over after track practice. I'm relieved she won't be over until six, because we won't have to leave school together. What would Paul's friends say about my hanging out with our school's only out lesbian? I picture us walking past the crowds and I hate to admit it, but it makes me nervous. It's weird enough to think that we'll know each other outside of school. I always thought of her as that keener girl who puts up her hand to answer every single question. I text Paul when I get to his house, to let him know I'm out front. A minute later, he comes out with a Pop-Tart in his hand.

"Seriously?" I ask when he opens the door. I nod in the direction of the junk food. "That's your breakfast?"

Paul smiles. He gets away with so much because of that smile. It makes me roll my eyes. We kiss and I put the car in drive. A fake raspberry smell wafts through the car.

"Are you excited about the game tonight?" he asks.

"Tonight?" *Oh crap.*

"Yeah. Canucks versus Mighty Ducks at Uncle Gary's. He asked us to bring chips."

"Uh," I stall. "I kind of forgot." I bite my lower lip.

"You said you'd drive."

"I know. I got the days mixed up."

"Well, what are you doing that's more important than the game?"

"English. Clea Thompson's coming over at six."

"Just tell her to come over earlier and we're all set."

"I can't. She has track and field practice."

He snort-laughs. "Figures," he says. He looks at me like I'll laugh along with him, but I don't find it funny.

"What do you mean?" I snap.

"Come on. She's a pretty classic jock lesbo stereotype."

"Don't use that word," I say.

"What? She is one. And proud of it, too. So what's wrong with saying it?"

"It was the way you said it."

"Just stating facts, but whatever," he says and scans the road in front of us. We're almost at school. "So can you meet her tomorrow instead?"

I shake my head. "She's really busy. We made plans and I don't want to cancel since it's the first time she's coming over."

"You made plans with me too, remember?"

"I know. I'm sorry."

"I can't believe it," he says. "I thought you wanted to watch the game."

"I would if I didn't have to study, but I'm

really stressed about school." I can feel the tension building between us as we enter the lot and I put the car in park. I don't want to argue. My stomach already feels like it's in knots over going to Mr. Davidson's class without having my homework done. Again. "Do you want to borrow my car tonight?"

"That's not what I'm mad about. I know you think I expect you to drive us everywhere, but I don't. I'm bummed that you don't want to spend time with me."

"I can't tonight." I'm firm on this. It's the only decision I can live with.

He sighs. "Sure, then. Why don't I drop you off at home and then take the car and I can pick you up before school tomorrow."

"Okay," I say. As much as he says it's not about the car, it is. Uncle Gary lives all the way out in Aldergrove. It takes about a century to get there by bus. My mom will be pretty choked about my lending out the company car, but she'll get over it.

"Kiss me," Paul says. I do.

***

After Paul drops me off that afternoon, I tear around the apartment making sure it's presentable. My mom's pet peeve is when I have people over and the place is a sty. I can already hear her complaining that my room makes her cleaning company look bad, as if any of my friends would really contract her company to clean. It's kind of hilarious. But I get it. I bet dentists' kids have to floss three times a day.

There is a knock at the door just as the oven timer goes off. When she comes into the apartment, Clea's cheeks are rosy. She has the athletic frame of someone who has been involved in sports from a young age. She's super muscular and not thin — the opposite of dainty. With her short hair and that build, strangers might think she was a guy. A good-looking guy, but a guy.

"Hey," she says. Her voice is deep and buttery rich.

"Come on in."

She enters the front hall of our apartment all eager, as if she's expecting to zip into the part of our home that most resembles a library. I should probably warn her that I mostly do homework on the couch in front of the TV.

"Where should we study?" she asks, taking off her dark grey hoodie.

"You have to eat first," my mom says from the kitchen. How embarrassing that she's listening in.

"My mom made lasagna," I say.

"Delicious," says Clea. "Alright. Fifteen minutes and then we hit the books."

"Holy taskmaster," I say half-jokingly.

"If we're going to work together, I need you to know I take everything I do seriously."

I don't think I can hide my shock. I might as well have invited Mr. Davidson himself over for dinner.

Mom pops her head out from the kitchen. "I like this girl," she says to me. Then she turns to Clea and says, "Come in. Sit down."

"Thanks, Mrs. Nussbaum."

"Oh, please. Call me Anita," Mom says. She's being unusually friendly, but I understand it. She drills Clea, wanting to hear about every award and accomplishment. It's embarrassing to me, but Clea doesn't seem to mind. As she lists each trophy and Principal's List award, my mom is so impressed that my heart aches with envy.

I turn to my mom. "Can you believe how lucky I am to get to work with her?"

"Very lucky," my mom agrees.

"It's not that big of a deal," Clea says, chewing madly, trying to keep up. Mom got her talking so much that we're sitting with empty plates in front of us while Clea's only halfway through dinner. I'm not sure she understands that to my mom, she's like a celebrity.

After dinner, Mom clears away the plates. "Why don't you two girls study here at the table. I'll put on water for tea. There's cheesecake in the freezer."

Mom is really rolling out the red carpet. She never offers cheesecake to Paul, and we don't usually eat dessert on weeknights. Clea opens her backpack and pulls out *The Great Gatsby*.

"So how much have you read so far?" She looks at me. Sweet, polite, mom-friendly Clea is replaced by Clea the drill sergeant.

"Uh . . . the title?"

Her expression tells me she thinks I'm an idiot. "Seriously? I talked to Mr. Davidson at lunch and he said we're almost through the unit."

"Are we?" *Phew! I'm looking forward to that.*

"That means tests and essays. Do you pay attention, like, at all?"

Okay, now that's just mean. "I didn't realize you came here to insult me," I say.

"Look, I don't mean to sound harsh but I'm getting a scholarship come hell or high water. Mr. D. told me he wanted us to work together because you're smart."

Wow. He said that? "And clearly you don't believe him."

"I'll believe it when I see it."

Ouch!

4

GATSBY AND BINKY

By the end of the hour, my mind is in overload. I feel like I've been introduced to a whole room full of people after Clea told me about all the complicated soap-opera relationships in the novel. I was planning on watching the movie, but she insists that's not good enough.

"Next time we meet you'll have read the whole thing, right?" she asks.

"In one week?!"

"It was assigned three weeks ago, so, yeah, you'll have to catch up."

"How do you make time to read so much?" I ask.

"So much? It's one little novel. You should see the stuff we're reading in some of my other classes."

"When do you do it?" *And how?*

"Well, it helps that I like to read. I just find a way to fit it in. After school. Weekends. You know." She shrugs like it's no big deal.

After she leaves, I clean up our dessert plates and think about how strange Clea is. I don't know if I like her or if I am afraid of her. It scares me half to death to think of letting her down. Once the kitchen is tidy, I take my book upstairs and open it up.

***

After the lunch bell, I head to my locker. Paul meets me there. He's holding a Coffee Crisp bar from the vending machine. He knows it's my favourite.

"For you, Binky."

"Thanks, Boo Boo," I say, hyper aware that the nicknames we use in private sound really stupid at school. I make a mental note to talk to him about it later.

He throws his arms around me and we kiss. Holding hands, we walk through the halls to the cafeteria. We pass Mr. Davidson's room. It's Thursday, so Interfaith is meeting. I glance in and spot Luanne sitting with Parm and Ranjit. I really miss Interfaith. But the thing about having a hot boyfriend is you have to hang out with him. If I don't, Brooke-Lynn Bradley will. Across the hall is Mr. Sidhu's room, where Clea is leading the Gay-Straight Alliance. There's something poetic about the fact that Interfaith and the GSA meet right across the hall from each other.

Forty-five minutes later, Paul and I are walking back from the caf as Clea is leaving Mr. Sidhu's room. I let go of Paul's hand and wave her over. "You two haven't officially met," I say. That's the thing with the busy and the popular — there's not a lot of intermingling. "Clea, this is Paul. Paul, Clea."

"Heard a lot about you," Paul says. "I hear

you and Binky are partnered up."

Clea looks at me. "Binky?" She scrunches up her face and laughs as if this is the funniest thing she's ever heard.

I want to disappear. "Usually just in private." I elbow Paul in the ribs.

"Ow," he says and puts his arm around my waist, pulling me in. He squeezes me really hard.

"Well, nice to meet you," Clea says as she walks off. "See you in English, Binky."

When I turn to Paul, he looks serious. "Why did you let go of my hand when you saw her?"

"Did I?" I ask. "Um, to wave, I guess. You know, like normal, friendly people do."

He nods. "Whatever you say. But you act different around her."

"Do not."

"Uh, yeah. You do."

"I just don't want her to think we're homophobic rednecks, you know."

"Whatever," he says. We walk back to my locker together, kiss one more time, and part ways.

***

That night I think a lot about what Paul said.

Determined to learn more about queer people, so I can be cool around Clea, I type some keywords into Google. Up pop tons of sites about bullying, frightening numbers for suicides among gay teenagers, and all kinds of tragic stuff that seems to have nothing to do with Clea. She's so together, so strong. Maybe I'm more prejudiced than I want to admit. There's so much I didn't know or think about. I want Clea to know that I accept her. *Should join the GSA?* If we're going to work together all year, it would be nice to spend at least a little social time with Clea.

5

JUST A GAME

On Friday night, Paul and I hit the strip in White Rock. In the summer, this place is packed with people from all over, but it's late October now. Even when it's cold, White Rock is one of my favourite places to go for a romantic stroll. We're out on the pier overlooking the bay when Paul grabs me and pulls me to him. He gives me a long, slow kiss.

"Want to get some fries?" Paul asks.

"Sure."

We go to Stella's. It's Paul's favourite place because they have bottomless fries and bottomless sodas, so for ten bucks we can both fill up on carbs and sugar and play some pool, too.

On the way there, he asks what level of Candy Crush I'm on now. I tell him about the latest rounds and how I stayed on the same level for five nights in a row, before finally breaking through to the next round.

"It's kind of obnoxious," I tell him, "because you're all obsessed with getting through this hard level and then you do and it's awesome, but you start on the next level and it's hard again."

"Don't overthink it, Binky. It's just a game," he says, squeezing my hand as we enter Stella's.

Inside, in a dark corner near the back, I see Brooke-Lynn and her pack of friends. Brooke-Lynn's in a miniskirt and her hair cascades down her back in perfect, long brown curls. When she sees us, she comes running over, all fake smile and bright, white teeth, and throws her arms around Paul. She gives him a European-style kiss on each cheek, like she's all sophisticated.

"Hey, guys," she says, beaming at Paul. She looks at me and her tone changes. "Hi, Sofie."

"Uh, hi," I say, wishing I could turn around and walk out the door.

"Come hang out with us." She looks right at Paul when she says it, as though I'm not even there.

"Sure," Paul says, as he grabs my hand and pulls me in the direction of Sandeep, Corinne, and Alicia. There is nothing worse than being held captive for a whole night watching my boyfriend flirt with Brooke-Lynn and her entourage. The girls laugh at his jokes and act dumb to impress him. He's either clueless or he likes stupidity or he just wants to be the centre of attention.

At one point, Brooke-Lynn compliments my hair in front of everyone. All eyes go to my freshly dyed red ends.

"Where did you get it done?" she asks. I know she's trying to make me look bad, but I won't play her game.

"My kitchen sink," I say. "Cherry Kool-Aid."

"No way," Sandeep screeches as she rushes to touch my hair. Before I know what's happening, they're all over me.

"My mom would never let me dye my own hair," Brooke-Lynn says.

I grunt. "Well, mine would kick me out if I spent two hundred and fifty bucks at a salon." *Like you.*

Two can play at the bitchy game.

"I guess we don't all have royalty cheques," she says, taking a sip of her Diet Coke. Darn her dirty diaper money. At least I didn't peak as a baby model.

"Anyway," I say, taking my time with each syllable, "who wants to shoot some pool?"

"Me," Paul says. We walk off toward the pool table. Finally.

Later that night, we're parked in my car, overlooking Crescent Beach.

"Can I ask you something?"

"Sure," Paul says. "Anything, babe."

"What do you see in me?"

"What?" He looks perplexed. "Why would you even ask that?"

"I just mean . . . I don't get it. I see the way you are with Brooke-Lynn and there's no way I can give you any of that." I probably should mention that Paul lost his virginity to Brooke-Lynn. And she's obviously still in love with him.

"Aww, Binky. Don't be insecure. You know I love being with you."

"But why?" *Especially considering I don't put out and I probably never will. In fact, it is very likely I will join a nunnery.*

"I dunno. Being with you is like hanging out with one of the guys, except you're a chick. I mean, we watch hockey together. You play pool. You're awesome. And smokin' hot. Brooke-Lynn and I are long over. Come here."

He pulls me to him and kisses me like that's all the explanation I need. Maybe it is. What do I know about love?

We're making out as Paul's hand inches

up my back. My skin tingles at his touch but when he gets to my bra and undoes the clasp, I sit up straight.

"What are you doing?"

"I . . . uh . . ."

"Look, Paul, I told you. I'm not ready."

"You're right, you're right. I'm sorry. Come back here," he says, doing up my bra again. He caresses my face. "I love you."

We continue making out, but after a while, he's the one who sits back and exhales like he's trying to calm himself down.

"We better cool it," he says, taking in a deep breath and letting it out again. "Let's call it a night before we do something we'll both regret."

I don't know what he's getting at. "Huh?"

"Just now. That was intense."

Was it? "Yeah," I agree. "It's late."

6

A GREAT TRAGEDY

The following week, I pull up in front of Clea's house, grab my school bag, lock the tin can, and check my phone again to make sure I have the right place. She lives in a nice house on Templeton Street. As I walk past the sculpted garden with little accent lights showing off the bushes and flowers, my heart begins to race.

Her mom answers the door. She looks me up and down, which only makes me more uncomfortable. "You must be Sofie. Clea mentioned you would be coming."

Mrs. Thompson looks like Nicole Kidman,

but with short, blond hair. Clea's features are darker. She mentioned being a "halfer," but I didn't know what she meant and it seemed impolite to ask. Then I see a family portrait on the wall. Now I get it. Her dad's black.

"Shoes off, please," says Clea's mom. "We just had the floors done."

The place is spotless. My mom would be impressed.

I kick off my Converse. I probably should have bent down to untie them. I'm giving a bad impression.

"Clea's in her room. Follow me."

"Thanks, Mrs. Thompson."

At first Clea doesn't answer her mom's knocks, so the knocks get louder. Finally, the door opens a crack and Clea pokes out her head.

"What?" she snaps, sounding annoyed.

"Your English partner is here."

"Hi," I say, stepping out from her mother's shadow.

"Sofie," her tone lightens. "Oh my God. I totally forgot. Come on in."

"Well, don't forget we have dinner with Ted and Janice at six," her mom says.

"I know."

"Have your application ready so Ted can look over it."

"I know!"

"Don't get snippy. It's going to look really good to have his letter of recommendation. He's doing this as a personal favour to your father."

"Okay, okay! I'll be ready," Clea shouts.

I wonder what it's like to have parents who know important people who will write reference letters. Clea gestures with her head for me to follow her in. "Let's hit the books." She sounds nicer as soon as her mom leaves.

"Wow," I say, looking around. "Cool room."

She has a few framed motivational posters on the walls and two huge bookshelves filled with books. Her bedspread is navy and the walls are grey. It's like being in a guy's room, but way cleaner and better smelling. I don't know where I should sit, so I stand.

"Thanks," she says, picking up some papers from the floor and bed. "Sorry, the place is a disaster zone right now."

"What a view," I say, and walk over to the bay window that overlooks a big backyard. "I could sit here and stare out this window for hours."

"Yeah," she says. "If only there was time for that."

Her laptop is open to a university website, but I'm too far away to tell which one.

"Where are you applying?" I ask.

"Everywhere," she says, closing her computer. "The early admissions and scholarship deadlines are coming up fast, so I'm kind of nuts right now. But enough about me, how are you doing with *Gatsby*?"

"You know, pretty good," I say, to my own surprise.

"Awesome."

"Yeah, I mean, I actually like it. I feel like I get Gatsby. I get why he wants to do better than what his parents expected of him, even though it goes horribly wrong. And I get Daisy too, how she did what everyone wanted and now she's miserable."

"It's a great tragedy." Clea nods, gesturing for me to take the chair next to hers. I take the seat and now we're sitting closer than usual. I'm hyper aware of it, but I don't move back. "Let's see your essay."

I'm suddenly nervous, sitting side by side at her desk. Our knees are practically touching. For some reason, it's all I can think about. I take a deep breath and remember why I'm here. This is the first time I have applied myself at school in a long time, maybe ever. I'm so afraid that Clea will see that I don't have the potential. She'll see that she was right the first time, and then she'll be disappointed that Mr. Davidson is making her work with me.

I fish out my notebook and flip through pages of doodles until I get to the essay. It's three pages long. Double-spaced and in large handwriting, but still. This might be the longest thing I've ever written.

"Let me take a look." She grabs the note-book. I feel naked.

I fidget as she reads silently. She looks at me, notices my nerves. "Here," she says, passing me a book. "Read this while you wait."

I look at the book in my hands. *The Collected Poems of William Butler Yeats.*

I flip it open and randomly read. "When you are old and grey and full of sleep / And nodding by the fire . . ."

Clea's the only person I've ever met who has poetry books stacked on her desk. She must really be into this sort of thing. There's nothing fake about her smarts.

I sneak a peek at her and she's nodding, so what I wrote can't be too bad. I look back down at the book in front of me. The poem is confusing, but by the end I realize it's a love poem. It makes me sad because I think I'm supposed to want to imagine growing old with Paul but I can't see it. Also, this Yeats guy has on rose-coloured glasses. He makes it seem fine to get old. Judging from the seniors I clean for, my guess is that it's brutal. Sometimes I'm their only visitor that week and they'd rather chat than let me run the vacuum.

"This is a good start." Clea turns to me. She puts her hand on her neck, like she's in pain. "I think you should rework the thesis statement and structure, but your ideas are good."

"They are?"

"Are you surprised?"

I don't want to admit that it's the first time anyone has ever told me my ideas are good, so instead I shrug. "I wasn't sure if I understood the book right."

"There's no right or wrong in literature. There are only interpretations and arguments."

"I'm pretty sure there's such a thing as wrong. I've seen a lot of X's in my life."

Clea begins to explain essay structure and the familiar hazy feeling is coming over me, but I do my best to concentrate. It's distracting me that she's massaging her neck and I finally interrupt her.

"Are you okay?"

"Huh?"

"Your neck."

"Oh, that." She seems self-conscious. "I think I pulled something earlier."

"What if you're really hurt?" Just looking at her, I sense the pain — and somehow it hurts me too.

One benefit to working for elderly people is they like to teach you cool stuff. I learned Reiki from a man named Nathaniel who studied with a master in Japan. I offer to try it on Clea.

"What's Reiki?"

"It's energy healing."

"Oka-ay," she says sarcastically.

"What?" I decide not to tell her about my credentials.

"Let's just say I'm skeptical." Her shoulders are tense. I notice how broad they are and how square. "I'm all about science."

"Well, just chill out and stop being a brainiac for once." My bossiness surprises me. I didn't know I had it in me to talk like that.

"Fine, okay."

I'm surprised at how nervous I am to touch her. She lets her arms drop to the side. I place my hands on her neck.

"Close your eyes, take a deep breath, and relax."

With my hands on her shoulders, I'm trying very hard to concentrate on healing, but her skin is soft and warm. I feel an intense charge as I touch her. It's unlike anything I've experienced before. Nathaniel taught me that Reiki is all about forgetting who you are, but I'm more self-conscious than ever. After about ten minutes, I sit back down next to her.

"You can open your eyes now," I say. Then I notice the trace of tears running down her cheeks, two thin, silent streams.

"Thanks," she says. "So anyway, back to your thesis statement."

"You were crying."

She nods. "I'd rather not talk about it."

"Try me."

"But your essay . . ."

"You already said it. I have some good ideas. That means I'll be handing in something better than anything I've ever handed in before. Let's not worry about my essay."

She looks down as though she's afraid to tell me what she's feeling. "I've never let anyone touch me before," she mumbles. "I didn't know it would freak me out."

"What do you mean?"

"I mean what I just said."

"But you're president of the GSA. I thought . . ."

"You thought what?" She looks at me like I'm some sort of hillbilly fool.

"I guess I thought if you were out as a lesbian, you must've made out with girls or something." I am rambling and I can't stop. I sound like a moron. Shoot me now.

"Well, the honest truth is no one has ever touched me like that before and I" — she chokes up and grabs a Kleenex from the box on her desk — "I didn't know I'd react like this. I'm sorry. I'm a stress case."

"Don't apologize."

"My neck feels better," she says as a kind of consolation.

"Sorry about what I said just now. I kind of figured you had a girlfriend or something."

"Like I have time for that. I don't have a life."

"Everyone has time for love if they want." Oh no. I sound like an idiot again.

"You have no idea the kind of pressure I'm under. Besides that, I don't think there's anyone around here who would be interested. Or, for that matter, anyone I find interesting."

"Hmmm," I say. "Lesbian matchmaking. I could be up for the challenge."

"No thanks," she says immediately.

I smile but I must have that mischievous look Paul tells me I get sometimes because Clea says, "Drop it, Sofie. Seriously. I am not interested." She says it slowly, underlining the point for me.

"Fine. I just don't like the idea of you being alone."

"Stay out of it," she orders. As if to regain control, she gives me another order. "Rework this. Try writing an actual thesis statement. I'll give you five minutes."

"Fine," I say and get to work.

7

AFTERLIFE

A few weeks later, Clea and I are in the study carrels on the second floor of the library, hidden behind a wall of reference books. Looking up from my work, I ask her if she's going to Grad. Paul and I got our tickets over a month ago.

"I'm boycotting it," she says with a sneer.

"Why?"

"It's a tired old tradition. Kind of silly when you think about it. I mean, my life begins after graduation."

"Yeah, but it's Grad." I shrug.

"Well, there's no way I'm showing up in

a dress. No way in hell. But wear a tux and be all alone in front of all these goons? No thanks."

I laugh.

"What's so funny?"

"You called everyone goons."

She laughs too. "Well, mostly everyone."

Then she says, "But seriously. Life begins after high school. This place is just glorified babysitting."

***

On Saturday, I pull up in front of Paul's house. It's an old split-level that looks like all the other homes on the street. Classic Surrey. It's not like fancy-pants Surrey where Clea lives or little-old-lady-ville where I live. This is where the seventies never ended. His dad's out pulling a blue tarp over their motorhome.

"Hey, Sofie," he says when he sees me. "Go on inside. Paul's down in the basement playing that zombie game."

"Thanks."

Paul doesn't notice me at first. He's shooting walking corpses with a gun that's connected to a huge, boxy television set. When he passes the level, I cough and he turns around.

"Oh, hey, babe," he says. "Come here."

He pauses the game and puts down the gun on the coffee table. His embrace feels good, especially after the week I've had, with so much reading and concentration. I just want to relax and enjoy myself.

We slump down on the floral-print velour couch and make out for a while. It's comfortable. Nice. For a second, I remember being at Clea's and how nervous I was sitting next to her, the electricity between us. It was as if I could feel her everywhere. Being close to Paul is easy. I realize in this very moment that he's my best friend. He offers me the second gun to the game, and we play for a while. Shooting zombies makes me think about death.

"What do you think happens after we die?"

I ask when we take a break to eat chips and Rice Krispies squares.

Paul looks at me like it's a no-brainer. "That's easy. Heaven."

"But what do you think it's like?"

He shrugs and tells me not to analyze so much. Hours pass. In the early evening, I feel a pain in my gut. The stomach cramps of guilt. The weekend is almost over and I promised Clea I'd do the grunt work on our upcoming video project, but I haven't even started.

"Am I gonna see you over the holidays?" Paul asks.

"Of course, but Clea said she'd help me with a bonus project for Mr. D."

Paul shakes his head.

I feel myself stiffen. We're headed for a fight. "What?" I ask.

"You, that's what. Remember the holidays last year? That was awesome." He touches my arm lightly and sends shivers up my spine. I remember. I was so crushed out on him that when he told me he liked me back, I thought I was going to faint. I didn't even believe him. We spent nearly every day together cuddling in my car, making out, and started the new year as a couple.

"I know — "

He cuts me off. "You've been so wrapped up in school lately," he says, like it's a bad thing.

"Well, it's a lot more interesting now that I'm paying attention," I say. *Really, talking about literature and life and what it all means is cool, and I'm doing well for the first time ever. Who knew that if you write from your heart, you can actually do well?* It's a shocker, but there's no way Paul would understand so I don't even try to explain.

In my room that afternoon, I'm trying to grasp what grammar is all about when I just can't take it anymore. Dangling modifiers. Run-ons. Fragments. I don't get it. I throw my school book on the ground. Nothing makes me feel quite as stupid as grammar. *Gatsby* was a breeze compared to this. I'll be lucky if I can even get a C in this unit.

Eff it. Time for Facebook, where nobody cares about grammar. I scroll through a bunch of updates, wondering what people are up to, noticing how many of my friends use "u" instead of "you," when something dawns on me. Paul's not the only reason I've lost touch with Luanne and my old gang. I've been so focused on reading and writing lately. No wonder Clea said she doesn't have a life. Studying takes a lot of time.

Clea doesn't usually update her status, but she did today. It says that she's taking a road trip to Washington and Oregon over the holidays to take a look at the universities there.

Before I even think it through, I leave a comment under her status. "Great! When do we leave?" I add a smiley face.

Clea told me she hates writing stuff on Facebook, but she uses it to keep in touch with a few people in the GSA and some of her old friends from Toronto.

She comments right away. "You want to come?"

I reply, "On a road trip? For sure!"

I stay tuned to my newsfeed for a while, but she doesn't write anything else. Eventually, I pick up the composition review worksheets again. Review? More like "never heard of any of this." Later, Clea sends me a private message with the details of her plans. It sounds like she wants me to come. My heart skips a beat thinking about what it will be like with just the two of us on the open road.

That night, Paul calls me. He doesn't even say hello. Instead, he says, "Really? You're too busy for me, but you have time to go on a road trip with Clea?"

Silence.

"Sofie?"

"I'm still here."

"Why don't you ever want to spend time with me anymore?"

"I do, Paul. I do."

"When?"

"I don't know. Now?"

I'm not getting anywhere with studying

anyway. I pack it in for the night and pick up Paul. We go for a drive and get hot apple pies at McDonald's and eat them in the parking lot.

Later that night, I knock on my mom's door, then open it a tiny crack. She's doing her evening stretches.

"Can I go to the States to check out universities?"

"You want to what?" She looks at me as if she doesn't believe what I'm asking.

"I'll be checking out Portland State University and the University of Washington and Western Washington University."

Her face is total confusion. "Really? Uh . . . sure."

"Awesome. Thanks."

"When?"

"Just for a few nights. Before Christmas."

"With Clea, I presume."

I nod.

"Where will you stay?"

"At her aunt's house." I don't mention that Aunt Sarah won't be there. Minor detail.

"Fine by me," Mom says. "What does Paul make of you spending so much time with Clea?"

"I'm not spending that much time with her."

I sound defensive and I know it. But really, what's the big deal?

8

ANOTHER WORLD

Clea buzzes at seven in the morning, as promised. I let her in. A couple of minutes later, she knocks at the bathroom door. I stop double-checking my packing to open the door.

"You're such an overachiever, you even have get to the border before everyone else," I tease, too excited to be groggy. My mom isn't even up yet. I can't believe we're really doing this. I barely slept. I was too excited.

"We have a long drive ahead of us."

"Not that long."

"Well, if we stop for lunch or whatever." She reaches for my duffel bag that's packed and ready to go in the hallway. She slings it over her shoulder. "I want to get there before dark."

"So let's hit the road," I say. I leave a note for Mom telling her that I love her and I'll text when we get there.

***

Crossing the border into the US is like going through a portal to another dimension. We live a ten-minute drive from the States, but it feels like a completely different universe. Clea plugs in her iPod.

"I made us a mix for the road. All kinds of weird stuff."

"Let's get coffee in Bellingham," I suggest.

"Sure."

Even at the drive-through Starbucks half an hour from home, the barista's accent is different.

We merge onto the I-5 and Clea turns up the music. We're singing along to old classics — Madonna, Culture Club, David Bowie. I love '80s music. Before we know it, we're approaching the outskirts of Seattle.

"Wanna stop for lunch?" Clea asks. "Or wait until Portland? I read about a place. I bet I can find it."

"Are you hungry now?" I reach into my bag and pull out the sandwiches I made. Prosciutto, basil, and havarti. I pass her one and she takes a bite.

"Oh my God, so good," she says as she chews. "But there's meat in them."

"So? You're not veggie, are you?"

"No, but we totally broke the law. You can't bring meat across the border."

"We're so bad," I say. "Like Bonnie and Clyde."

She smiles. We eat.

We go back to singing. I offer to take a turn driving, but Clea says she's fine. By the time we pass Seattle's suburbs, I feel like a different person.

"The world is so full of opportunities," I say, eyeing the random businesses along the highway, ma-and-pa restaurants, satellite stores, and trailer parks. "Sometimes in Surrey it feels like there's only one way to do things."

"Nope. There are infinite ways." Clea points out a sign for a taxidermy shop. "Like that, for example."

"Back home it feels like there are so few options."

"That's just because you associate home with being in high school. There's so much to do with your life," Clea says. "Most of the time I'm overwhelmed by the possibilities."

"That's because you're good at everything."

"I'm not always good at stuff."

"Then you sure know how to fake it."

She looks offended. "I don't fake it. I'm interested in most things. You could leave me in a field for three days and I'd probably find something to study. You know?"

I nod my head, but I haven't ever felt that way. Gazing out the window, I try to imagine a stranded Clea, notebook in hand, counting spiders and mice.

We pass a sign that tells us we are now in Oregon. Portland is complicated, but Clea's skillful behind the wheel. She doesn't even use the GPS system.

We get to Northeast Portland and turn onto Alberta Street. Clea manages to park right in front of the Tin Shed. The café is really cool and so full of awesome characters and their dogs that we have to wait in line.

A lanky guy with a big, lopsided beard and a baseball cap seats us near the back.

"It's awesome here," I say. We have nothing like this back home.

"Totally. It's pretty close to the university and I want to scope out where I'd be spending my time if I move here."

"Why do you want to go so far from home?" I ask.

"Because I can," she says, like it's the most obvious reason in the world. "My dad's American, so I have dual citizenship. And I don't want to run into anyone from high school."

"You really hate them so much?"

"Not everyone. The GSA people are fine. The teachers are pretty good. I'm just so sick of standing out. I need to find out where the other freaks are, so I can blend in with them."

I look at her. She's never used a word like *freak* to describe herself before. The trip is bringing out a new side of both of us. I glance around. "This place is promising."

She nods.

"For the record," I tell her, "I don't think you're a freak."

"Probably means you are one yourself." She winks then takes a bite of her veggie burger.

I think about what she said as I eat silently. I've never been happier to be far away from home. On our way out, a girl with bicycle-chain earrings and a buzz cut on one side of her head and long, curly blue hair on the other hands Clea a flyer.

"Y'all should come tomorrow night," she says, smiling. I'm shocked that she thinks that we belong at the same event. She looks at least two or three years older than us. Then again, I did vamp up my coolness with my side ponytail; big, hot pink plastic hoops; and the frayed Pink Floyd shirt I got at the Sally Ann.

Clea thanks the girl, takes the flyer, and tells her that we're visiting from Canada to check out the university.

"Well, who cares about that?" the girl says, laughing. "I mean, yeah, go check it out. The party's not till later. Come." She winks at Clea.

"Maybe," Clea says.

"If you don't, I'll be disappointed." The girl pouts, then flashes a pearly smile. "I'm Zelda. Hope to see you there."

Clea nods.

With that, Zelda disappears back into the crowd of gorgeous people in the Tin Shed.

9

THE COOLEST

We pull up to Clea's aunt's house off Killings-worth just as the city begins to grow dark. It's barely evening, but it's freezing cold. Clea finds the key her aunt left for her under a pot-ted plant and opens the door.

She shivers as we enter. "Aunt Sarah must have turned the heat off when she left."

"Yikes," I say through chattering teeth. "Do you know where the thermostat is?"

"Nope."

We haul in our bags and lock the front door. Freezing, I clasp Clea's arm as we search the house. Finding the central switch in the kitchen, Clea cranks the heat. We hear a roar, but we're still shivering, so we start to jump up and down. I take her hands in mine and exhale onto them, trying to warm her up. Then I hug her. She doesn't say anything, just stands perfectly still. I remember how she reacted to Reiki and fear I've overstepped an invisible boundary. After a moment she puts her arms around me, too. Even though we're freezing I feel warm next to her.

"Let's make tea," Clea says, moving away from me and heading to the counter. She fills the kettle and opens the cupboard. Inside is every kind of tea imaginable: loose-leaf herbal and black teas in jars, wire balls to put the tea in, and about thirty different boxed teas.

"Holy," I say.

"Yeah. She hosts a lot of book club meetings and stuff like that, she once told me. I've been down here in the summer, too, and she's always got people stopping by."

"Cool."

"Yep. She's the coolest. She teaches in the

Women's Studies department. Last summer we were hanging out making jam when Carrie Brownstein dropped in. She was really nice."

"No way! I love *Portlandia*. That's incredible."

"Not really. The queer community is pretty small and tight here. I guess that's why I want to check out the university. Seems like a great city."

I didn't realize Clea's aunt is also queer — or Carrie Brownstein, for that matter — but now that I look around, I notice the walls are decorated with paintings of women and there is a rainbow magnet on the fridge.

In the living room, we put down our steaming mugs on the coffee table. Clea takes a neatly folded blanket from the back of the couch and offers me one part of it.

"I'm so glad you let me come with you," I tell her. "I had no idea how trapped I felt at home until we left. I feel free here."

She nods. "I get it. I'm feeling that way myself."

"And about English, I seriously can't thank you enough. I feel like I finally understand stuff that I never thought I would get." Not dangling modifiers, but I don't bring that up in case she wants to start explaining them right now.

"It's my pleasure. Honestly." She sips her tea and glances around. "Can I tell you something?"

"Of course."

"Before I got to know you, I always thought you were snobby."

I'm taken aback. It's the worst thing I could hear from her. "You did?"

"Sure. You're blond and pretty and I guess I thought that made you one of the popular girls who would never lower themselves to talk to me."

"Are you kidding me? You're way cooler than I am," I say, shocked at what she said. "Seriously. You're athletic, smart, and president of the GSA. I thought you were too cool to talk to me."

She shakes her head. "High school is so stupid. I hate all these fake divisions between people. We could have been friends a long time ago. Now we're practically already out of there. Imagine if Mr. D. hadn't put us together. We would have moved on and never known anything about each other."

"That's the saddest thought ever. Thank God I'm dumb. Because we all know that's what that new program is really all about, pairing up the dense and the dazzling. Hey, that should be a soap opera."

I expect her to laugh, but she looks serious.

"Don't say that." She looks me right in the eye. "Don't ever put yourself down like that."

"Well, it was true until you came along."

"Knock it off. You're one of the smartest people I know."

I feel tears welling up that I can't hold back. "No one's ever told me that before."

"Seriously?"

I nod.

"High school is pathetic if it can convince someone like you that you're not smart."

I'm stunned and speechless.

"You know what?" Clea says. "I have no idea what you want to do with your life. What's your plan?"

"I dunno. Graduate?"

"After that."

"My mom wants me to take over her business someday, but I can't really see that happening."

"If you could do anything, what would it be?"

"Anything?"

"Anything at all."

"But I can't do anything I want. And there's nothing I'm really good at."

"That's not what I'm asking. I'm asking: What would you do if you could do anything you wanted?"

I know the answer. I've just never said the words out loud before. I never thought anyone would be interested in knowing, not even Paul. I take a deep breath. "I'd become a chef.

I love food. I love cooking. I'd have a food cart or a little restaurant or something."

Her eyes light up. "That's perfect. I can totally see it."

"You think?"

"Uh, yeah," she says with a hint of sarcasm, like I'd be a fool not to go for it. "Those sandwiches today? Amazing!"

"I mean, I'm glued to the Food Network. I can't get enough of cooking shows. And whenever I'm stressed out, I go to the kitchen and make something. As soon as I'm chopping or whipping or blending, I feel way better."

"You're like an artist."

I smirk. "Don't make fun."

"I'm not. I mean it. Cooking is an art, isn't it?"

"I dunno. Never thought about it that way."

"Well, think about it. You need skill and discipline. Some people are born with talent, but you also need training. And people who really love what they do are unstoppable."

"You should be a career counsellor."

"Nah. Then I'd have to work at a high

school." She pretends to stick her finger down her throat and makes a retching sound.

"It's so weird that you hate that place, too. Paul says he hates it, but that's just because he's failing and he says his teachers suck. I actually think he loves it, roaming the halls, surrounded by girls. Everyone wants to be his friend. But you — you rock at school. You're like this superstar and yet you really hate it."

"Brave front."

"You're obviously pretty good at pretending. I thought you loved it."

"I love the teachers. I love learning. I can't stand being trapped with all those . . . What did we call them? Goons."

As we unpack and change into pajamas, I can't help but think about how great it feels to be here with Clea. About how much I like her, and how amazing it is that she seems to like me.

I look around the room I'm staying in. Clea's aunt has a huge poster on the wall that says "Free CeCe McDonald" along with a ton of photos of herself with her arms around people at protests and events. There's a desk with books on civil rights and Audre Lorde and Alice Walker scattered all over the place. Apparently, she has this fantastic life as a researcher and instructor, which is why she is out of town right now. She's at a Women's Studies conference with a title I didn't catch.

Clea calls for me to hurry up and join her downstairs. "Your aunt seems so cool," I say, coming down the creaky wooden stairs of the small heritage house. "She has a great style."

"Yeah, she's awesome. I wish you could meet her."

"And she's a . . . lesbian?" I don't know why I hesitate. I guess I don't want to label anyone I don't know.

Clea doesn't seem to notice. She nods. "Aunt Sarah made life way easier for me. I mean, part of why my parents weren't so shocked about me is because she broke it to them a long time ago. She's a great role model."

10

WHEN IN PORTLAND

We check out the Portland State University campus the next day. Walking around with our paper cups of coffee feels very grown-up. No one looks at us like we don't belong. Clea's busy looking at empty lecture halls and classrooms. I'm scoping out the fashion of the few folks who are on campus. People here are so much cooler than the ones at home. Maybe it's because they're older, but there's this kind of individuality about people here. A "wear what you want to wear, be who you want to be" vibe. It's amazing.

"PSU was voted the most gay-friendly

campus in the States last year," I tell Clea, reading stats off my phone.

"Why do you think I want to check it out?" She reveals a coy smile.

"Aha! I knew you weren't all about the studies all the time. Busted!"

She shrugs. "I have to get a girlfriend sooner or later. Figured I'd go where the odds are best."

"You would rule the school here," I tell her. It's totally true. Even right now, in this very moment, she looks like she owns the place.

She grins. "How cool would it be to get a scholarship here?"

"Very cool," I say. "So, hey, are we going to that party?"

She looks undecided. "Do you want to?"

"Hell yeah."

***

The party turns out to be huge. It's at a club called Holocene and the people there are even cooler than the ones on campus. It's hard to believe that this is what a queer crowd looks like. I realize right away that I must have had some stereotypical ideas in my head because if I were plunked down here by aliens, I'm not sure I'd guess that these people are any different from the people I've seen back home — except that they're way cooler. It's high time I join the GSA. I wonder if Zelda thought Clea and I were together. It's hard to describe how that makes me feel but the word that comes closest is *flattered*. That and *nervous*. We get our age-defining bracelets from the bouncer, so we can dance but not drink.

Clea's being her usual shy self, barely able to look around. She's wearing a navy sweater vest with a checkered shirt and pink bow tie. Why she wants to hide in the corner of the room is beyond me. She's easily the cutest girl here. Clea should be out flaunting it, but I guess that's not for me to say. We hang out and watch the crowd for a while, but as soon as a song comes on that I recognize, I grab her hand and pull her to the dance floor. She does not want to go.

"Come on," I tell her.

Once we're dancing, she seems to tune out the crowd. We focus on each other. We lip-synch to the song. I'm on top of the world.

The DJ mixes in a slow song and suddenly it's way more awkward than that time I went to the school dance in Grade Nine and a slow song cleared the gym. Clea and I look at each other. Neither of us knows what the other person wants to do. But there's no way I am going to let this moment end.

Over the music, I yell, "When in Rome!"

She smiles.

I take her hands and place them on my hips and then I drape mine around her shoulders. It's like yesterday when we were hugging in the kitchen, but now we're in public. This time we sway to the music, soaking in the energy of the room. The song seems to play for a really long time.

***

In the bathroom, I see Zelda. I thank her for inviting us and tell her we're having a great time.

"Cool," she says. "If you guys end up at PSU next year, you should get involved in the femme collective. Us femmes gotta stick together, right?"

"Femmes?"

"Yeah, you identify as femme, right?"

"I'm not sure." I'd seen the word online, but no one I know had ever used it.

"Sorry if I made an assumption. You two were so cute yesterday."

"Thanks," I say.

"Are you going to be moving down here too?"

"No," I say. "Just Clea."

"How long have you been together?"

"Since October," I say, shocking myself. Where did that come from? I know perfectly well she's not talking about English class.

"Are you guys exclusive?"

What does that mean? "Uh, no?"

"Good to know," Zelda says. "See you back out there." She checks her teeth in the mirror, smiles once more, and leaves.

In Portland, I'm free. For the first time ever it's clear to me that I've been living up to everyone else's expectations of who and what I am. All this time, I've never looked inside, never asked myself: Who am I?

The word *femme* feels right to me. As soon as Zelda leaves, I whip out my phone and look it up. Feminine lesbian. Queer femme. Man, I really have to get myself to a GSA meeting. There is so much to learn.

In the middle of a public washroom, my life suddenly makes sense. I'm not the person everyone at home thinks I am. Somewhere deep inside I must have known, because I have always felt like an outsider. For the longest time I thought maybe it was because I'm half German — or an only child, or I have a single parent, or I'm left-handed. But it's deeper than all of that. I quickly flip through Google images of femmes, girls in rockabilly retro dresses, girls with heavy eyeliner like mine. Girls with attitude. Girls who inspire.

I stare at myself in the mirror. A large tattooed girl in a red leather dress washes her hands in the sink next to me. I don't know her but I feel connected to her. Maybe she senses it because when she reapplies her lipstick, she tells me she thinks it's my colour. It's bright red. She asks if I want to try it.

"Sure," I say and put it on. I look in the mirror again. I am on fire.

Rushing back out to the dance floor to find Clea, I am dizzy with excitement. In my head, I'm already packing everything I own into a moving van and bunking with Clea in a dorm next year. This is where I belong. These are my people.

"I love Portland!" I yell above the music.

People turn and stare but I'm all smiles. Clea laughs and shakes her head at me like I'm nuts. Maybe I am.

We dance into the early hours, not just with each other, but with everyone. Zelda finds us on the dance floor and we bounce around together. It's incredible how friendly this place is, and how fun. The rhythm of the music comes over me. I am finally clear on why Clea consumed my thoughts all those nights at home. Never in my life have I wanted to kiss someone as badly as I want to kiss her right now. Whether that makes me bisexual or lesbian is anyone's guess. I once read that *Q* can stand for "questioning" in the alphabet soup that makes up LGBTQ. I don't know what letter I am and it doesn't matter. Dancing with her is like spelling it out in neon: I have a crush on Clea. I keep repeating the sentence in my head, inching ever closer to accepting the truth.

At two in the morning, we leave the party. Back in the car, Clea gets a playful look in her eyes.

"Let's go to Voodoo Donuts," she says.

"What's that?"

"Oh my God. It's the best." She pulls out of the parking lot and turns on the radio. A song we'd just danced to comes on, so she rolls down the windows and blares it. Even though it's the middle of winter, we're still hot from dancing and the breeze feels divine. Part of me is nervous we'll be pulled over by the cops, but another part of me just wants to sing at the top of my lungs.

We arrive at a funky-looking donut shop. It's the anti–Tim Hortons. It's painted black and the girl serving us has a massive nose ring like a bull's and blond dreadlocks dyed green.

"Two Canadians," Clea orders.

The girl's tattooed arm reaches into the glass unit in front of us. She pulls out two maple-glazed donuts, each with two strips of bacon on top.

"Whoa," I say when Clea passes one to me.

"Try this, my foodie friend," she says.

I bite into the sweet, savoury goodness. "Oh my God."

"Right?" Clea says. "Delish."

I love seeing this new side of her. The way she talks here — she's totally out of her shell and it's the greatest thing ever. It's crowded but we manage to squeeze into a dark corner where there are two stools side by side. Sitting down, I shake my head in disbelief.

"This is the best thing I have ever eaten in my whole life. Ever."

She laughs. "Glad you like it."

"You really know your stuff."

"What can I say? I love eating."

The overwhelming urge to kiss her comes over me again. It's like some kind of magnetic pull. I am able to control myself, but barely. I think this is what Paul meant that time in the car when he needed to stop making out because it was too intense. I didn't get it, but now I do. This is intense. I feel like I need a time out to bury my head in a pillow and scream, but I doubt it'd do any good. I focus on the donut and concentrate on the flavours mixing in my mouth. Even my palate is in overload.

11

BIG QUESTIONS

There is no way to undo it. I could try to hide my crush on Clea, but it doesn't seem right. Looking out at the street flooded with beautiful people, I have this crazy image of inviting her to Paul's and my wedding in a few years and her showing up with her fabulous Portland girlfriend. Even the thought pierces my heart. I can't live without her. And I know for sure now that I can't be with Paul.

We drive back to her aunt's and make ramen. She turns on the TV and we catch the end of a zombie flick, huddled up with our bowls of instant noodles on the couch.

She slurps her soup. "Sometimes it feels like people back home are all like this." She gestures at the screen.

"Surrey zombies," I say in a creepy horror voice.

"Surrey zombies . . . Sombies!" She laughs. We're on a total sugar and adrenalin high.

When I'm finished, she takes my bowl and stacks it on hers on the side table.

"Time for bed?" she asks.

I don't want to be alone yet. "I'm not tired. Can I ask you something?"

"Sure," she says.

"What do you think happens after we die?"

"Where's that coming from? Everything okay?" She puts her hand on my forehead as though checking for a fever.

"The zombies got me wondering."

"Well," she takes a deep breath. "Maybe we become worm food. Maybe there's nothing."

"I never understood that — the concept of nothingness. That's part of why I failed Science last year, actually. I asked Mr. Stetic what was beyond the universe and he said there was nothing. After class I asked him what he meant by nothing. I guess he thought I was making fun of him because he hated me after that. But I still don't get it. I mean . . . nothing. What's that?"

I'm rambling, so I stop and say, "You can tell me to shut up any time."

"No, no. I've thought about that, too. Nothingness. How our minds are literally incapable of understanding it. Like, sometimes I wonder what the hell is up with black holes, you know?"

I nod. "Oh my God, yes! They're so freaky."

"Part of me can't wait to get into the sciences at university. According to my brother, they actually talk about stuff like that. Like emptiness and that. High school sciences are so boring. Just memorizing stuff."

"I hated it." And I also failed to memorize anything.

"Yet you think about black holes and what lies beyond the universe."

"I watch documentaries. Okay, true confession. I'm a huge nerd in private. I just can't remember any of the details and I don't want to take tests that make me feel stupid."

"So you let your hatred of studying hold you back from the big questions? I don't get you sometimes."

Defensively, I tell her about the times I felt like I wasn't smart enough or good enough. I explain how I've always believed I wouldn't do well at school and how that's only just starting to change now, only because of her. But then I realize I've yammered on about myself for too long and I'm not the only one around here with issues.

"Well, what about you? With all your poetry books and memorized Shakespeare passages and all that."

"If I could just study literature all day every day, I would be about a million times happier."

"So why don't you?"

"Please," she says like the answer should be clear. "I'm from a family of engineers."

"So?"

"So, literature is a hobby at my house. A pastime. It's not a career." She says the last sentence in a stern, parental voice.

"It's your life. When you're worm food, won't you want to have lived it to the fullest?"

"Are you saying I'm not?"

"No. You said it. You'd be a million times happier. Well, I'm not the greatest at math, but I know that's a lot."

We're both yawning but fighting sleep. The antique clock on the mantel tells me we're closer to sunrise than sunset. But for some reason, I'm determined to stay on this couch, leaning on Clea. I've never felt so close to anyone before. If I were to die now, I have at least had this moment. This is the kind of night that makes life worth living. I put my head on her shoulder. She rests her head on mine and pulls the blanket up to cover us. After a long while, we fall asleep.

It's six in the morning when Clea guides me up the stairs and ushers me into her bedroom.

By that point, I'm more of a zombie than the ones in the movie and I keel over. She spoons me as I doze.

I wake up to the winter sun shining through the bedroom window. I'm all alone, but there's a scent of coffee wafting through the air. Suddenly, a light knock at the door.

"Wake up, sleepyhead."

Clea comes in with a hot mug of coffee.

"What time is it?" I ask.

"Noon."

"Seriously?" I sit up, alarmed. I was out cold.

"Well, we were up pretty late."

"Last night was awesome," I say, taking the mug from her. I blow at the steam. She's already put cream in the coffee for me, and probably sugar too. She remembered. "You have to go to school here next year so I can come and crash with you."

"Sounds like a plan." She sits down on the bed next to me. I prop the pillow up against the wall and lean back. She says, "You snore."

"Do not!" I insist.

"Oh, you do." Her eyes widen as she says it.

"Did I keep you awake?"

"No, you just made me laugh this morning."

I'm mortified. "How long have you been up?"

"A couple of hours," she says. "Long enough to watch you sleep, do a couple of Sudoku puzzles, and read the PSU catalogue I picked up yesterday."

"Wow."

She shrugs. "Want breakfast?"

I nod.

"Let's go out for brunch after you finish your coffee."

"Totally," I say, then I take another sip.

I've always fantasized about being a fabulous person who goes out for brunch. Portland rules. Clea rules. Suddenly everything rules.

***

Driving home along the I-5, I know nothing will ever be the same again. I look out over the landscape whizzing by us, cold and barren, though not covered in snow. There are so many evergreens, but it's the other kind of tree that captures my attention each time I spot one, naked and bare. We drive in silence for a while, both of us sipping lattes we picked up before getting on the highway.

I glance over at Clea. "Can I ask you something?"

"Sure."

"If you've never kissed a girl, how do you know you're queer? I mean, like, really know, like, for sure." The words sound so stupid. I don't know why I asked.

"Sofie, that's sort of offensive. I mean, I don't question your right to be straight."

"I'm not talking about rights. I think it's great you're queer."

Oh. My. God. I am making the biggest idiot of myself right now. I should confess. Be naked like the winter trees. Tell her I'm thinking about myself, not her. How do I know for certain? And what the hell do I do about Paul? And how do I tell my mom? And how will my life change? "I guess it's just that I'm curious about . . . well, I never thought that . . ."

"That what?"

"Never mind." I can't say anything. Not yet. I don't know how to tell her that I understand how she knows, because now I know myself. So I don't.

Instead I say, "I love the way my jean jacket looks on you." I told her to try it on this morning and she's still wearing it. It suits her.

"Really? Thanks."

Clea smiles. The awkward moment is over. Lesson learned: when you say something embarrassing, bring up fashion to change the subject.

"It's yours," I say. "Keep it." She really does look better in it.

"Thanks. But at least let me pay you for it."

"No way. I got it at the Mennonite thrift store for, like, four dollars."

"Seriously?" Clea checks herself out in the rear-view mirror. "Cool. But hey, don't ever mention that part to my mom. She'd freak out if she knew I was wearing something second-hand."

"Are you serious?"

"Uh-huh. Haven't you noticed? She's a total brand-name whore." Clea shakes her head. "She loves dragging me to the mall. She wishes I was more girlie."

"You don't have to be girlie to love shopping."

"Oh God," she rolls her eyes. "You sound like her."

"Well, the lady's offering to buy you stuff. What's the problem?" I'd give anything to have a mom who actually wanted to buy me stuff. My mom's only interested in paying off the mortgage."

Clea focuses on the road ahead and she seems stiff. "You have no idea what it's like, do you? Who am I kidding? Of course you don't. Look at you."

Huh? "What are you talking about?"

"For someone like me, shopping is a nightmare. The saleswomen give me funny looks. They always want to take over and make me try on stuff I'd never wear in a million years. If my mom's there, she gets all excited and they gang up on me. At first I can defend myself but I get weak after a couple of hours. That's when they strike and I find myself taking a skirt or a dress into the change room, where I have a mental breakdown. You have no idea how many times I have cried at the mall."

At first I think she's joking, that there's no way anyone would treat her like that. But the more I think about it, the more it makes sense. Those saleswomen are awful. They usually treat me as if they think I'm going to steal something. And Clea definitely does not look like she's interested in a dress, but try explaining that to the programmed Sombies.

"You wouldn't cry if I was with you."

"That's never happening," she says in a

solemn tone. "You and I are never — and I mean never — going to the mall together."

"Fine," I say. "If you want to keep suffering, go ahead. I'm just saying, if you and I went together, we'd have fun. I know we would. I'd even take you to the badass thrift stores where the sales clerks are elderly ladies who do needlepoint right at the cash register."

She flashes me a look like she's curious.

"You're missing out. I'm telling you, I'm an excellent shopping partner." I'm doing my best to charm her. I can't stand the thought of anyone making her uncomfortable. She's gorgeous. People can be such idiots.

We listen to music for a while and then Clea says, "Her name is Tionda. I was madly in love with her in Grade Ten. That's how I know for sure."

"So what happened?"

"My dad got a job. We left Toronto. I didn't have the guts to say anything to her. We're still Facebook friends. She's got a girlfriend who's nothing like me at all so maybe it was for the best."

"Wow. Must have been rough."

"Yeah. I took one look around in Surrey and realized no one else was like me. Since then I've thrown myself into school and track and . . ."

". . . getting the hell out," I finish her sentence. She nods.

I go back to singing along with the music and look out at the landscape, reading all the road signs. Then, as though I see a deer on the road in front of us, I yell, "Pull over! Take this exit!"

Clea obeys. Then she shouts, "What the hell!"

"Up ahead," I say. "Outlet stores." I grin at her.

"You have got to be kidding me. I thought you were having some kind of medical emergency."

"It's medical in a sense. We're going to heal your fear of shopping."

She protests, but we are officially on a mission.

We rummage through Goodwill and some big-brand stores, decking her out in a whole new wardrobe, all well-fitting, super cool stuff, mostly from the men's department.

12

CHRISTMAS DECORATIONS

When we cross back over the border, there's a lump in my stomach as I think about going back to real life. I hate real life. I want to stay away forever. I want to be the person I've been these past few days: self-assured, spontaneous, alive. I don't want to go back. I never knew how much everything sucked because I didn't have anything to compare it to. Portland is Shangri-La.

More importantly, I realize that everything I was obsessed with until I got to know Clea was so superficial. I finally know that being popular with Sombies has no meaning. I would rather walk my own path, which leads me to a far bigger question: Where am I going?

***

Christmas comes. Mom gives me a prepaid gas card. I give her a scarf I bought in Portland. I give Clea a beret I knitted and she says she loves it. I'm surprised that she also has something for me. She gives me a book of poems by Rumi, her favorite poet. I clutch it to my chest. I can't wait to read it.

And then there's Paul.

"The men are setting up the movie," Mrs. Smith says when I show up at Paul's on Christmas Day.

His mom ushers me into the kitchen where she and Paul's sisters, Chelsea and Laney, are heating frozen cheese puffs and sausage rolls and making deep-fried stuffing balls.

"I helped pick out Paul's gift to you," Laney says. "I hope you don't mind."

"No, of course not," I say. "That's nice of you."

"He's so hopeless when it comes to getting stuff for girls."

His mom chimes in, "No one wants him to repeat the Brooke-Lynn fiasco."

Chelsea says, "Seriously, is there a single girl in the whole world who would want her boyfriend to get her toenail clippers and socks?" She shakes her head.

I had no idea he gave her that. I try to imagine Brooke-Lynn on the receiving end but I just can't. It's funny to think about, though.

Downstairs, Paul is watching *Ultimate Fighting Championship* with his dad and Chelsea's and Laney's boyfriends when we interrupt with trays of goodies.

"I thought you boys were setting up so we could watch *Elf*."

"Don't get your knickers in a knot, dear," Mr. Smith says. The guys all laugh. "We're ready."

He clicks a button on the remote and up pops Will Ferrell in green tights.

"We've watched this every year since it

came out," Laney whines. "Can't we watch something else?"

"But it's so funny," Paul's mom says. "It's a Smith family tradition."

Family. The word chimes in my mind like a pinball ricocheting. I will miss the Smiths. There's heaviness in my heart as I think about how I'm going to tell Paul about my crush on Clea. Can I even tell him? He holds his hand out to me and I take it. He pulls me toward him, so we're sitting close together on the couch. Then he puts his arm around me.

Every time the room fills with laughter over the movie, I get this pain in my gut like I'm some kind of destroyer of dreams. I feel like a fraud, pretending things are funny and light. I think about all those nights my mom sat up late drinking wine at the kitchen table before she told my dad it was over. She must have known in her heart that it was over, but had not been able to say anything. I get that now.

After the movie, Paul takes me by the hand and leads me upstairs to his room. I sit cross-legged on his bed. He lies down beside me and then rolls over to pull open the drawer in his nightstand and produces a little green-and-red wrapped box.

"Merry Christmas, my love."

I wish there were something wrong with Paul. Anything at all. He's the perfect guy. It's awful.

"Thanks," I say with tears in my eyes.

"I hope you like it."

I will the words to come out of my mouth. I want to tell him everything about Clea and the word *femme* and how it calls me to be the real me. What kills me is if we weren't in a relationship, I could totally tell him. If it were just us, back in math class last year, two random people who just kind of clicked, I could pour out my heart to him. If I had known back then, we could have avoided this misery.

Instead, I open the present, very slowly, like each fold of paper weighs a thousand pounds. I can't hurt Paul. I love him. Maybe I don't love him the way I might be able to love Clea, but I love him. I can't say anything. Not yet.

Beneath the wrapping paper, there's a purple velvet box with hinges on one side. My pulse races. I hold the box in my hand so long that Paul must know something is up.

"Open it," he says.

I do. It's a silver locket shaped like a heart. Inside there are two tiny photos of us together — one taken at Playland last summer and the other of us roasting marshmallows that time we went camping with his parents.

"Oh, Paul." I start to tear up again.

"I thought you might like it."

"I do," I say. "I do."

Whether his sister helped him or not, this is the sweetest present he could have gotten me and I don't deserve it at all. I'm a faker. A liar.

"I got you something, too," I say. "I put it under the tree downstairs."

"Right on," he says and zips off to get it.

I stay on his bed, clutching the locket in my hand, unable to put it around my neck. He comes back with my present to him and tears off the paper.

"Yes!" he shouts, holding up the Vancouver Canucks jersey. "You're the best girlfriend ever."

"I hope it's the right size."

He puts it on. "Perfect," he says, "like you." He kisses me.

"Let me help you with the necklace." He opens the clasp and fastens the chain around my neck. It feels like I'm wearing a flashing sign that says "Faker." A noose.

13

BROKEN UP

I can't keep up the masquerade much longer. On the morning of the twenty-seventh, I wake up in a cold sweat knowing that the day has come.

I text Paul and ask if I can come over.

Paul's mom passes me a tray overflowing with cookies. "We got so many tins of baked goods from people at church this year. Please, Sofie, help us eat some."

I reluctantly place a snickerdoodle on a red and green napkin.

"Want to play one of my new games?" Paul asks.

I'm pretty sure he can guess I'm not in the mood to shoot enemy alien intruders. "Can we talk instead?"

"Okay." He doesn't budge from the living room sofa.

"In private?"

"Um . . . sure."

I follow him to the basement where the video game is paused on a still image of an alien clutching his heart as he dies.

"What's up?" Paul asks.

"I've been doing a lot of thinking and I feel like our lives are going in different directions." It's the best reason I can come up with short of telling him about my feelings for Clea, which I'm still tempted to do. It depends on how he takes it. You really don't know someone until you break up with him.

"Oka-ay . . ." he says, taking my hand. Paul looks concerned.

I take a deep breath. "I mean, we're growing apart."

I stare down at my lap. The cookie looks

revolting and instead of eating it, I want to throw up.

"You're breaking up with me?"

I sit perfectly still, not knowing what to say. Everything I rehearsed at home seems stuck in my throat. I can't speak. I start to cry.

"How long have you known?"

"Not long, Paul. I swear."

"Holy shit, Sofie," he says so quietly I can barely hear it.

"I'm sorry."

"Is this about Brooke-Lynn? I can tell her to back off."

"No. It's not her."

"What is it then?"

"I don't know," I say. "My feelings changed."

"You don't love me anymore?"

"Part of me will always love you, but I can't be with you anymore."

"I can't believe you. And at Christmas."

"I'm sorry," I repeat, not knowing what else to say. He's right. It's the worst possible timing. But my feelings don't operate on a set schedule.

"You should go."

"Really? Are you sure?" I wonder if maybe I should stay so we can talk more. Or maybe we should just hang out quietly together like we sometimes do. All of a sudden, I'm the one who's not ready to accept that I've put an end to the incredible year we've had together.

"You're my best friend, Paul," I manage to say.

"I don't want to see you," he says. It hurts more than I imagined.

He looks more angry than sad as he sits back down, fixating on the controls of his game. He won't look at me again. I can tell.

"Are you going to see me out?"

"Goodbye, Sofie," he says.

Upstairs, his mom calls from the kitchen. "What are you two up to today?"

"I was just leaving," I say.

"So soon? I wondered if maybe you want to go to the mall with me, so I can get some attachments for my new KitchenAid."

"No thanks, Mrs. Smith."

She comes around the corner to where I'm lacing up my shoes.

"Sofie, you're crying. What's the matter?"

I gulp. "We broke up," I tell her.

"Oh no!" She tugs at her cardigan. "Can't you work through it, whatever it is?"

I shake my head. "I don't think so."

Tears are streaming down my cheeks now and I'm embarrassed by the way I ruined their holidays.

Back in my car, I manage to get out of Paul's driveway despite my blurred, teary vision. As soon as I'm out of sight of the Smiths' house, I pull over and sob into my steering wheel.

I feel empty. It's the exact opposite of the high I felt a few days earlier in Portland. Here, I have nothing. I mean, truly nothing. Paul will never forgive me for breaking his heart and neither will his friends at school. I'm going to feel like a horrible person for the rest of my life, so no one will ever love me. And it's not like I know what's up with Clea, whether she would ever like me the way I like her. It feels like I've caused an earthquake and everything is in ruins.

I cry until I'm shivering. Then I turn on the ignition, letting the heat blast at me until my eyes are clear enough that I can drive again. I don't go home. I'm not ready. Instead, I drive to the beach and look out at the water. I think about true nothingness. When I'm worm food, or in heaven, I'll probably be glad I followed my heart. But right now I feel like the biggest loser who ever walked the planet.

***

On the first Monday back after the holidays, I cringe in the familiar hallways, like an escapee who got out and is now back in jail. Paul and Brooke-Lynn are the first people I see as I'm walking toward my locker. I smile and offer an awkward wave at Paul, but instead of acknowledging me, he looks right past me as though I'm not even there.

Brooke-Lynn comes right up to me. "Stay away from him."

"I was just . . ." . . . *waving to the guy I still love, just not like that.* Not that it's any of her business.

"Go clean a toilet, bitch. You've done enough to hurt my man."

Oh my God. Her man?

Paul takes her by the arm and pulls her away. "Come on," he says. "Let's get out of here."

I'm stunned. I can't believe how quickly I was replaced. No wonder Paul didn't bother to return my texts or calls.

At lunch I see Luanne, but she's busy with her other friends. As usual, she blows me a kiss from across the hall. It feels like the fakest thing ever. How our friendship ever turned into these gestures is beyond me, even though I guess I'm at fault.

I eat lunch by my locker and pretend to do

homework. On Thursday I am definitely haul-ing my butt to the GSA. No question about it. I open the poetry book Clea gave me to a ran-dom page and read a line. "Why do you stay in prison when the door is so wide open?"

It's a really great question. I want to leave the school, my old identity, everything I know.

When the three o'clock bell rings, I rush back to my locker, anxious to leave the op-pressive, crowded hallways. A note tumbles from the top shelf and lands on the textbooks down at the bottom. I open the envelope and read the two words written in Clea's hand-writing in purple felt pen.

"You're beautiful."

For a split second, the world is a friendly place again. Clea likes me, too! It's fate. I'm soaring above it all. I clutch the note to my chest and feel like swirling around surrounded by sparkles and glitter like a Disney princess. Then I notice the girl next to me has the same note and so does the guy a few lockers down.

What the . . . ?

I hear people talking about the GSA's sweet outreach project. My heart sinks. I'm not special. She doesn't like me like that and maybe I'm a fool for ever thinking she could.

***

When I meet Clea at the library later, she's practically blushing, and her eyes are fixated on her phone. She looks so cute, and I want in on whatever she's enjoying.

"Zelda found me on Facebook and we've been chatting."

My stomach flops. I'm going to barf. This is the worst news ever. "Oh?"

"Yeah. She's so cool. She's studying film at PSU and she said if I come down again I can stay with her and she can show me around."

I'll bet. "Great."

"We've chatted only a few times, but she already told me she thinks I have a great smile."

"No argument from me," I say. Clea looks

up. She seriously has no idea how she lights up a room. It's like she's never looked in a mirror. Zelda's just stating facts.

"Thanks for insisting about the party. I probably wouldn't have gone if you hadn't encouraged me."

"No problem," I say through clenched teeth. "Haven't I always said I wanted you to find love?"

"You have." She's downright giddy. "And now it's happening!"

I sigh and look down at my books. Anything is better than watching Clea swoon, even studying.

"You know what's weird, though?" Clea asks. "At first when Zelda contacted me, she said she thought that you and I were girlfriends. Isn't that hilarious?"

"Yeah," I say, but I'm not laughing.

"She must have misunderstood something you said, because she said you told her we were."

"Did I?" I ask innocently, even though I

remember clearly. "She must have been confused."

Now I know what Zelda meant when she asked if Clea and I were exclusive. Well, I want to put a locket around Clea's neck, and tell the whole planet that we exclude everyone, especially fashion-savvy girls from Portland. "Not to be all keen or whatever, but can we get back to Shakespeare?"

"Oh, right. Sorry."

Clea reads my *Twelfth Night* stage directions for the scene we have to perform in front of the class. I'm pretending to read, but like usual, I am watching her closely for clues. She nods the whole time.

"Sofie," she says. "Are you sure you want us to do Olivia and Viola's lines in front of everyone?"

"We totally have to."

Clearly, Shakespeare wrote a romantic scene between two girls almost five hundred years ago just so we could perform it.

"You're a brave one, Sofie Nussbaum."

Maybe so, I think, but I'm no film student with a cool, blue buzz cut. This day blows.

Unable to sleep that night, I go to my computer and Google "gay" and "Christian" together. Hours pass. There's so much to read. It's worse than Candy Crush.

14

TRUTH

Later that week, I'm hanging out alone in my room — again — when I finally know what I have to do.

"Mom?" I knock at her bedroom door and open it a crack. She's reading a romance novel, which usually isn't the best time to catch her for a serious discussion.

"What is it?"

I take a deep breath. "I want to surprise you on Sunday. Instead of regular church, I want to take you somewhere else."

"Oh?"

"Say yes."

"Alright."

"Thanks, Mom. You're the best."

She gives me a look that tells me she agrees. Then she looks down at her book again.

***

Thursday lunch hour finally comes. I walk into Mr. Sidhu's room, where people are already eating their lunches.

"What are you doing here?" Clea asks.

"Can I join?"

"Anyone can." Her bland response surprises me. I thought she'd be excited to have me in the GSA. But then I see she's busy setting up the DVD player. Just when I'd started to think of her as a regular person, I remember she's actually the president of this club.

I take a spot near the back of the room. These last few days have been pure hell. I've been so alone. I think about the saying that goes something like, "Friends are strangers you haven't gotten to know yet." As I scan the room, I fight back tears. I was getting so sick of eating lunch all alone by my locker. It overwhelms me to think there are probably other people who feel the exact same way. I force the tears to stop. There's no need to frighten everyone at my very first meeting.

***

A couple weeks later, I text Clea to see if she wants to hang out on a Saturday night.

"Sure," she replies. "Come over for dinner?"

I obsess over it for the rest of the week and wear my church clothes. I bring dessert, so Clea takes me right into the kitchen where her mom is putting the finishing touches on a roasted chicken dinner.

"Pavlova!" Mrs. Thompson says when she sees it. "How exciting."

At dinner, Mr. Thompson tells us about a bridge project he's working on. When I tell him that it sounds cool, he asks if we want to visit his office. I say I do.

Clea's brother, Kurt, tells us all about second-year engineering at a university in California. He's back home healing after a sports-related injury, but his passion for the courses is pretty cool. It's like listening to Clea talk about poetry.

Mrs. Thompson turns to me and asks me the question I fear the most. "So, what do you want to do after high school?"

"I don't really know yet. Clea's trying to get me to follow my heart."

"Where does your heart want to go?"

"Culinary school."

I thought she'd look disappointed, but instead, Mrs. Thompson gives me a supportive smile and says, "Well, I think that's fabulous."

"I'm working really hard on pulling up my grades. Actually, Clea's kind of changed my life."

Clea tries to downplay the compliment. She's been telling me how her parents always criticize her and tell her to work harder and do better. I can't help but want to tell them how great she is, which is why I persist.

"It's true," I say.

"You've been doing the real work," Clea says.

"Yeah, but you made me believe I could do it. Actually, without you, I'd probably be failing and there's no way I'd ever consider going to culinary school."

Mrs. Thompson says, "Well, it's great to have goals for yourself." She pushes out her chair. "I'll put on water for tea. Who wants dessert?"

Everyone at the table digs into the pavlova and the conversation is replaced with "mmms" and "ooohs."

"Delicious," Mrs. Thompson says.

"It's surprisingly easy," I tell her.

"Wait a second," she says. "You made this?"

I nod.

"I don't even make desserts like this. What a treat."

"I love baking," I say.

In Clea's room later, she asks me if what I said about her at dinner was true.

"Yes," I say, sitting down on her bed. "One hundred per cent. I don't know where I'd be if you hadn't come into my life."

She sits next to me. "Same here. You made me see that there's more to life than competing for first place and getting out of here. And you remind me to have fun."

I stare her bookshelf. "Clea?"

"Yeah?"

"Remember how you told me you never thought you'd meet someone at our school worth kissing?"

"Yeah."

"Do you still feel that way?"

"What?" She looks perplexed.

I clear my throat and take a deep breath. This is it. The moment of truth.

"I haven't been able to stop thinking about you. I mean, like, at all. I fall asleep thinking about you. I wake up thinking about you and you're on my mind all day. I know you've got this thing with Zelda or whatever and I don't really want to . . ."

"Are you coming out to me?"

"Um, more than that actually."

"Oh my God, Sofie." She shakes her head like she can't believe what I'm saying.

I take her hand, but I suddenly feel dizzy. My stomach is in knots. My mouth is dry and my hands are trembling.

"Sofie," she says gently. "I had no idea."

"Really? None?" I take shallow breaths. "Because I've been feeling pretty see-through lately, especially when you talk about Zelda."

"Zelda's just a . . ." She looks away. "I don't know. A friend. A flirt. Someone to gush about while everyone else talks about boy-friends and all that."

"I don't talk about those things."

"I know you don't. That's what makes you so cool."

Cool. She thinks I'm cool. What does that mean? "So you're not in love with her?"

Clea shakes her head and I feel so much

relief I can barely handle it. "She's sweet and I like chatting with her online, but she's not . . ." Clea grasps my hands in hers. She looks right at me and says, "She's not you."

"You mean . . . ?" I'm almost shaking.

She nods. "From the first time you came over. I thought I was doomed to be one of those sad lesbians who falls for a straight girl."

"No, you're not," I say, reaching up to touch her cheek. "I've been trying to find a way to tell you."

Her dark brown eyes are watery. We have never stared into each other's eyes like this and I know why. It's kind of frightening. It's like she can see right into the depths of my being. I'm exposed. Open. Scared.

"Clea?"

"Yes?"

"I've been wanting to kiss you since Portland."

"You have?"

I nod. "Yes."

We're so close I can feel the heat coming from her body. I lean in, but she jerks back. "Wait. Maybe I should go brush my teeth. I've been dreaming about this moment for a long time."

"You're adorable," I tell her. "This isn't a test. You don't have to get everything perfect."

She closes her eyes and leans forward. For a split second I find it kind of hilarious that I'm the experienced one. I've kissed one other person. But I'm completely unprepared. I take her hand and it's shaking slightly. Sensing her nervousness makes me even more nervous. Even holding her hand is something I never thought would happen. I lean toward her. Our lips barely brush against each other — whoa. Fireworks and sparklers! Shooting stars and rockets! This is not like anything I've ever experienced before and it feels so right.

15

OUT

Sunday morning, I'm up, dressed, and pouring freshly brewed coffee into two commuter mugs. Mom drinks hers black. Mine is practically half cream and there are three big scoops of sugar in it. Breakfast of champions.

"Where are you taking me?" Mom wants to know.

"You'll see when we get there."

I drive. We cross the Nicomekl River and merge onto Highway 99, heading for Vancouver.

"Are we having brunch?"

"No," I say. "Well, maybe later."

"So, where then?"

"I told you. It's a surprise."

After an hour of driving, I pull into the parking lot of an old Gothic church on Burrard Street.

"I've always thought this building was so beautiful. It reminds me of Europe."

"I know, Mom," I say. She says it every time we're downtown. "We're here."

We walk in together and find a spot to sit down. The minister comes in wearing rainbow colours and Mom looks at me, puzzled.

"Something new," I whisper. Silently, she turns to face the front of the church. I watch her from the corner of my eye. She's shifting back and forth, clasping and unclasping her hands. When the sermon is over, we shake hands with our nearest seatmates and then leave. Mom is stiff as we exit. It isn't until we're in the car again that she exhales.

"Sofie." She turns to me. "Are you trying to tell me something?"

"It's time for a change, Mom."

"Are you . . . ? Do you prefer this church? I

mean, belong at this church?"

"Yes, Mom. I do."

She looks out the window and says nothing. Her face is turned away from me and I'm pretty sure it's because she's crying. I pass her a napkin I'd shoved into the pocket of the door one day when I picked up a drive-through meal.

"That minister in there? He's been married to his partner, a man, for more than twenty-five years," I say. "His husband was the first openly gay ordained minister in the United Church and he was the second."

Nothing but sobs and the back of her head.

"His husband's a politician. He's on city council."

All impressive stuff in my humble opinion — but still nothing but sobs.

"I don't know what you're upset about. I thought the sermon was great and you said yourself that you like the architecture."

"That's not the point." She sniffs.

"Mom, I'm not trying to hurt you."

"I know, Sofie," she whispers. "I know."

I figure brunch is out of the question, so I pull out of the parking lot and head back to Surrey. On the way home, Mom says nothing. Then, as she's taking off her seat belt, she says, "I liked what he said about God never making mistakes. There are no mistakes."

"Me too."

"I just don't want your life to be any harder than it has to be." She begins crying again as she says this.

"Well, the only one making it hard for me right now is you."

I regret the words as soon as they're out. I might as well have slammed a door in her face. I just don't know how she can take it so personally. It's not about her.

Once we're home, she goes to the washroom and closes the door. I hear the bathtub fill. She's probably covering up the sound of more crying. Clea never even had to tell her parents. They figured it out with Aunt Sarah's help. How cool would it be to have an aunt like that? But on the other hand, there's a guy in the GSA who says his parents would kick him out if he told them. So, I guess I'm kind of lucky.

About an hour later, I'm in my room, looking at YouTube videos of narwhals when Mom knocks on my door.

"Yeah?"

She opens the door, comes in, and sits on my bed.

"Sorry if I'm freaking you out," I say.

"Sofie," she says in her most serious voice. "You're my daughter and the only family I have."

She's being dramatic. We have plenty of relatives. She just doesn't talk to them. I wish I could take back today. It was probably a lot to spring on her all at once.

We sit in silence for a while. I look at her. She returns my gaze and finally says, "I like Clea."

I want to tell her that we're not technically an item — not yet, anyway. It's too new to tell what we are, but this is probably the closest I'm ever going to get to the "I love you and accept you just the way you are" talk, so I don't want to ruin it. I lean forward and nod.

"Thanks, Mom."

She gets up, pats me on the head, and leaves.

I go back to watching footage of a pod of narwhals making their way through a corridor of water, in between broken patches of sea ice.

***

Later that week, Clea and I are standing by her locker when I hear someone near us cough then spit out the word "dykes" in our direction. Clea pokes her head up for a second and says, "Idiot." I wonder if her quick reaction is a sign that she's had to defend herself against that word before. I don't have time to ask. I'm late for class.

I look for Mr. Sidhu after school. He can tell something is up because I don't usually crash a teacher's classroom and I've only been to a couple of GSA meetings so far. He looks up from the papers on his desk and asks me what's on my mind.

I sit on top of one of the desks near him, convinced I won't be able to talk, when all of a sudden it just pours out of me: Paul, my mom, Clea, my plans for the future. Everything. I even admit something I'm ashamed of now that I'm in the GSA. I tell him that I'm afraid of being labelled.

He puts down his pen, opens the top drawer of his desk, and takes out a Coffee Crisp. My favourite.

"My wife only lets me eat sugar a few times a week, so this is special for me. I'm going to share it with you because you just shared so much with me." He breaks it in two and passes me half. It's the best chocolate bar ever.

Then he says, "You know, I don't think we ever get away from the fear of labels and being different. It's human nature to want to be part of a community. That's why excommunication and solitary confinement are such brutal forms of punishment."

Leave it to a history teacher to bring in stuff like that.

"I never thought of it like that before."

He continues, "Labels can be a way for others to feel as though they have authority over you. But they can also be a powerful means of understanding your identity in the world."

"So you're saying I should wear the words as a badge of honour?"

"That's what I do. When I was your age, it wasn't that cool to be the Sikh guy at a mostly white school. But I'm Sikh. I was always Sikh. It's my identity and my community. I had a choice way back then. I could either try to conform, or I could accept myself."

I think about Clea and what she told me about having no choice but to accept that most people would guess she's queer. That's even more true now with the clothes we picked up in the States. She told me she can actually feel people making up their minds about her after just a few seconds. I don't know what that's like.

"What's weird is that I don't think anyone

can tell about me," I say. "I mean when I'm by myself. It's like I'm invisible or something."

"You're not. I see you."

"But you wouldn't think I was queer unless you knew me, would you?"

"Sofie, invisibility is a superpower. Never forget that, okay? I used to long for that back when I played with the Marvel gang, which of course I never do anymore." He flashes a smile. There are superhero figures and posters all over his classroom. "The point is, I didn't have a choice in how people saw me then and in a way I still don't. But you do. So what are you going to do about it?"

I think about how calling myself queer might mean that some people treat me differently, but it'll also mean I can find my community. It was so easy in Portland. That one word helped us to know exactly where to go.

"Thanks, Mr. Sidhu."

"Any time." He gives me a nod and I know our little session is over.

16

CONSEQUENCES

It's Wednesday, and for once Clea doesn't have any kind of club, sport, or activity at lunch, so we eat together. No matter how much time we spend together, it doesn't feel like enough. I almost want to take up track or Calculus — almost. It feels like we understand everything about each other and the more we talk, the more we have to talk about. We head from the cafeteria through the crowded hallway of people jostling each other, hurrying to their lockers. It's noisy and the corridor smells like gym bags and perfume.

Clea leans in and whispers to me. Ever since that night at her place when we kissed, all I can think about is tucking my face into her neck and breathing in the orangey sandalwood scent of her skin. But we're subtle at school. The truth is, I don't really know what we are to each other. Neither of us has said the G-word yet, so we're not girlfriends. Now she tells me she wishes we were back in Portland, not here surrounded by the Sombies.

The first face I see when she says this is Mr. Stetic's. His dandruff always falls onto my homework when he's leaning over me in Science. It makes sense that he's a Sombie. Maybe he's even the leader.

The thought cracks me up, so I tell Clea and now she's laughing too. We huddle like that, giggling in the middle of the crowded hallway.

Then, out of the corner of my eye, I see Paul and Brooke-Lynn. She glares at me like I'm some kind of ogre, then she laughs as if she's looking at a caged animal performing a trick.

Paul isn't laughing at all. His eyes shoot daggers at me as he shakes his head and walks past.

Later that afternoon, in the middle of English, my phone vibrates in my pocket. It's Paul.

"We need to talk."

"Thought you weren't talking to me," I shoot back. I hold the phone in my hand and two seconds later, it buzzes again.

"I'm serious, Sofie. Meet me at our spot after school."

He means the hedges behind the gym, outside next to the field. I haven't been out there since before we broke up and I don't know if I can stomach it.

The rest of English is awful. It's not Mr. Davidson's fault, but I can't hear a word he's saying. All I can think about is what's going on in Paul's head.

When I get to my locker, Paul's there waiting. I thought I'd be able to check my hair first and maybe go to the washroom, but nope. It must be even more urgent than the text made it seem.

"Hey," he says. He looks grim.

I follow him out to the field. He's in his soccer uniform and I see him now the way others see him. He's no longer my Paul. He's Paul, the golden boy. Paul, the soccer player. Paul, the drool-worthy, popular guy who every girl wants. Every girl except for me, that is.

"I'm glad you want to talk," I say. "I miss your friendship."

"To hell with friendship, Sofie. I want answers. Are the rumours true? Are you in love with Clea Thompson?"

"Define love."

He glares at me and kicks the bike rack. I stand back for a moment, reminded of the temper I'd so quickly forgotten about.

"I never meant to hurt you," I say quietly. It's the truth, but I'm not sure he is ready to hear it. "I can't change who I am, Paul."

"I can't believe you." He shakes his head. "You didn't even tell me."

"I wanted to, I just couldn't."

"What the hell? What happened?"

"I can't explain it. Something just clicked."

He shakes his head. "But I mean, when we were making out, you were into it, right?"

"At the time, yeah."

"And then you woke up one morning and you were into chicks and the thought of me was revolting?"

"No, Paul. It was nothing like that. It's just that, I dunno, I think of you more as a friend." *My best friend, actually.*

"What bugs me most is being completely blindsided."

I want to tell him that he didn't do anything wrong and he shouldn't blame himself. I want to tell him that I didn't hurt him on purpose. Instead, I just stand there, silently wondering what happened to the sweetness that was once between us. I couldn't possibly feel further apart from him than I do right now. I'm broken-hearted, too. However, he wouldn't believe me if I said it, so I keep it to myself.

"I'm sorry," I repeat.

His tenses up again and the look in his eyes

is fierce, like a ferocious lion. He shocks me when he clenches his fist and kicks the bike rack once again, his temper telling him to take out his anger somewhere.

"Sorry isn't good enough. Brooke-Lynn was right. You're a bitch, Sofie Nussbaum. You can't just mess around with people's feelings like this."

With that, he walks away. I watch him, stunned. I've seen angry outbursts before, but nothing this hateful. I wish I had never met him, wish I'd never gone out with him, wish I could believe without a doubt that I didn't ruin him. Maybe I did. Maybe I'm a horrible person.

I watch him walk away. On the other side of the field, in the distance, I see Brooke-Lynn. She's so far away, it might not even be her. I hope it's not her. It's time to go home. I stop at Save-on-Foods to pick up some dark chocolate, blueberries, and flour. This day calls for scones in a major way.

***

The next day, I'm walking down the hall past Brooke-Lynn and her friends' territory. Naturally, they all have their lockers together. They're looking my way.

Suddenly I hear, "No wonder she couldn't keep him satisfied."

I turn toward Brooke-Lynn. For a second I'm convinced she's going to pretend the comment was not aimed at me.

"Hello?" I say quietly. "I'm right here."

Her friends all stand behind her, staring at me. She's puts her hand on her hip like she's practised modelling poses in front of the mirror, like she's trying to be Kate Moss. She advances toward me.

"I don't care what you are — gay, straight, whatever," Brooke-Lynn begins. "None of my business. But it is my business when you have a romantic little meeting with my boyfriend."

Romantic? What?

"Brooke-Lynn, I never . . ." My words fail me. She's staring at me the way an eagle probably looks at a field mouse before it swoops down and snatches it with its talons.

There's no way to explain the situation to Brooke-Lynn, so I don't even try.

"You can't have both of them," she says. "There will be consequences."

She turns around as if she's on a runway, but there's nowhere to go. She faces her friends, ignoring me. I guess the conversation is over. There's nothing left for me to do but leave. I continue down the hall to my locker.

Once I've got my stuff crammed into my backpack, I slam the locker door closed and click my combination lock together. As I'm leaving school, I check my phone for messages and that's when I see it.

On Facebook some person named Har Lee pops up in my notifications. She or he said something about one of the photos I'm tagged in. I click on it. It's last year's Interfaith club photo from the yearbook. Luanne uploaded it a long time ago and I'd forgotten all about it, but now there's a comment by Har Lee. All it says is "Dyke."

What the hell? Is it Brooke-Lynn? Paul? Some random hateful person? I can't delete the comment beneath the photo, but Luanne can. Once I'm in my car I call her.

"Sofie?" She sounds surprised to hear from me, which makes sense.

"I've been a lousy friend," I blurt. "I'm sorry I haven't called. I'm sorry we lost touch. Can we talk?"

"Sure. Come for fro-yo," she says. "We're at Menchie's."

I don't know who "we" is, but I say okay. It's a short drive.

When I walk in, Luanne's there with Parm. They're almost finished. I don't bother with dessert. I just sit down in one of the white plastic chairs.

"What's up?" Luanne says. "I haven't seen you in, like, forever."

"I need your help." I pull my phone from my back pocket. "Can you delete this?"

She takes my phone, reads the comment, and raises her eyebrows. "Who is Har Lee?"

"It could be anyone."

Parm grimaces and shakes her head. Luanne whips out her phone. She fidgets a bit, clicks around, then looks up and says, "Done."

"Thanks," I say.

Crisis over. Now I'm ravenous for frozen yogurt. I grab a bowl and swirl in chocolate and original Greek yogurt. Then I hit the toppings bar and load up on cookie crumbs, jelly worms, and chocolate sauce. I pay and sit back down.

Luanne says, "I've been meaning to call you."

"Same," I say. "I've missed you."

"Tell us about Clea." It's almost as if the last year and a half of us drifting apart didn't happen and we're back to being besties. I know she knows that Clea and I are more than just friends. If it's obvious to Brooke-Lynn, it's got to be completely transparent to Luanne. Before long, I'm gushing about everything to Luanne and Parm.

17

CANDY CRUSH

Clea and I are still not officially an item. Maybe it's because we're both too freaked out about change. It was like this with Paul for the first month or so, too. It's as if the butterflies are too much. To name what's really happening between us is impossible. Every time Clea and I see each other in the hall, it's like we're both shiny balloons filled with helium, floating above it all.

I'm in my room playing Candy Crush. Clea sends me a text that interrupts my game.

"Is it true that you met up with Paul?"

"What?!" I text back. "Who told you that?"

"Just tell me whether or not it's true."

Uh-oh. This is not the kind of conversation to have via text. I call her. "Just tell me who told you," I plead. "I need to know."

"Some fake account on Facebook," Clea says, clearly annoyed. "Har Lee."

"Oh my God. I think it's Brooke-Lynn. Or maybe Paul," I say. I can't believe this is happening.

"You still haven't told me whether it's true," Clea says.

"Technically," I begin.

She cuts me off. "That's all I needed to hear."

"Clea. Wait."

"I've got shit to do, Sofie. Provincial exams to ace. Projects to complete. I don't have time for this. I thought you were into me."

"I am." *More than anything!*

"Well, you have a funny way of showing it."

"It was nothing. Paul and I were saying goodbye. As in forever."

"Whatever. What hurts is that you didn't

tell me. I had to find out from some dumb-ass Sombie."

"You're right," I say. I want to apologize, but she's two steps ahead of me.

"Look, I need some space for a while. Let's just cool it with everything, okay?"

She is off the phone before I even have a chance to explain. I'm in my room, clutching my phone, all alone and stunned.

I call Clea back, but she doesn't answer.

I know she's at Robotics Club. My instincts tell me to get into my car, drive to school, and force my way back into Clea's heart. But I'm almost certain it will backfire. She told me she wants space.

Overcome with guilt, I pace back and forth in my room trying to figure out why I didn't tell Clea about that afternoon with Paul. Why didn't I? What was I afraid would happen?

I call her again. Still no answer. I can't just stay here and do nothing. I get into the tin can and head toward Clea. Then I wander the halls second-guessing myself. What if this is it? What if it's over between us?

I find the Robotics Club in a classroom in the Science wing. Peering through the slim, rectangular window in the door, I spot her right away. I knew she wouldn't leave the club meeting. She's engrossed in some kind of group project and her back is to the door. I'm still not sure it's a good idea to burst in on her like this. What am I going to say? I touch the doorknob then turn back around. There is a row of lockers beside the classroom, so I lean against the cool steel for a moment, weighing the possibilities. If she rejects me, I might leave here with nothing. But if she forgives me? I have to know. I brush the beads of nervous sweat from my forehead and take a deep breath. Then I open the door to her classroom. The guy she's working with sees me and gestures. Clea turns.

When she spots me, she gets up and comes to the door. Her eyes tell me she's not happy I'm interrupting.

"Can I talk to you?" I ask.

She seems distant, but she steps out of the classroom anyway. The hallway is empty and it has an echoing quality. It's almost spooky.

"I should have told you," I say. "I need you to know you're the one I have feelings for. It was always you. Since before Portland."

"Really?" She pouts as if she's not convinced.

"Please believe me. Paul and I were saying goodbye. Anyway, I'm way too hung up on you to even think about anyone else."

"You are?"

I throw my arms around her. "Totally. I never meant to keep it from you. It was stupid. I was insecure."

"Well, don't do it again. All I want is for you to be honest with me. We need to be able to trust each other."

I nod. She brushes my cheek, sweeps my hair away from my face, and kisses me.

I can't control the tears that well in my eyes. "I just want to be good enough for you. Sometimes I feel like I'm not."

"Sofie," Clea says, holding my hand. "Don't say stuff like that."

I shrug. "It's the truth."

"I'm proud to be with you," she says. "I mean, be seen with you. Be, you know, like, close."

"Is that what we are? Close?"

Clea looks down. "I've been meaning to ask you something properly. It feels like I should since I made a big deal about being the butch and all, but I'm, uh, hell, I'm shy. I thought I could put this off until college."

Everything about her is adorable, especially her shyness. This is the girl who leads meetings, wins races, gets awards, is constantly mentioned in the morning announcements, but right here, right now, she is so vulnerable. Like me.

"You know I'm gonna say yes," I say.

"I'm shy."

I clutch her hand. "Just ask."

She looks into my eyes. "Sofie Nussbaum, will you be my girlfriend?"

"Yes."

***

Life with a girlfriend is awesome. For a few weeks, we're in our own little bubble. I don't care what any of the Sombies make of us. All is well in my world.

Then one morning while I'm getting ready for school, I check Facebook and see that several of my so-called friends — Paul's friends who didn't delete me — are going to an event called After Grad. It's hosted by Har Lee. I click on the event and see a picture of me that's been Photoshopped to look like some kind of horror show with the tag line "Don't Let This Ruin Your Grad" scrawled above it. In the invite, it says After Grad is the "real" grad party.

I don't want to go to school. I can't face this today. The knots in my stomach hurt too much.

I'm barely inside the school when Mrs. Choldenko, the vice-principal, comes out of the office and stops me. "You're Sofie Nussbaum, right?"

"Yes."

"Have you seen the Facebook event called After Grad?"

"Uh-huh."

"Listen, I'm sorry, Sofie. We take this sort of thing very seriously. We have a strict anti-bullying mandate, as you know."

She obviously wants to make me feel better, but it doesn't work.

"We're going to address this during announcements and force the culprit to come forward. I'm sure someone at the school knows who is behind this."

"Oh God. Please don't."

"School policy," she says. "And don't you worry. We'll punish whoever did this."

That's it — I snap. I turn on my heels and walk out of the school. Mrs. Choldenko calls after me, but I'm not turning back. No way. I get into the Sunny Side Cleaning-mobile and burn out of the parking lot. I can't handle being there. I'd die if I had to hold my head up high during announcements.

I drive to Esquires and buy myself a mocha with extra whip. I inhale it and then buy another one and inhale that too. Now I'm jittery and my stomach is cramping. I take out my school books and decide that I'll study at the coffee shop. At least until first period is over, then maybe I'll brave it. But I can't concentrate. I slam the book closed and drive back to school. I have to face this. There is no way out. But when I turn into the parking lot, my stomach is in knots and I can't do it. I pull into the lot, then follow the cement barricade all the way around until I'm out again.

I drive down to the beach and park on the strip. At this time of day, there are plenty of spots that don't have parking meters, so I can stay here all day if I want. I pull a lever to push my seat back all the way, so that it's resting on the back seat. Then I turn off my phone, grab my sunglasses from the glove compartment, put them on, and use my jacket as a blanket. In spite of all that caffeine, I fall asleep.

I don't wake up for over an hour and when

I do, I get out of the car and walk along the misty-grey beach until I'm completely soaked from the rain. Hours pass as I look out to the waves for clues as to how to deal with this mess.

18

LIPSTICK AND FREEDOM

After school, I check in with my teachers to find out what I missed. The halls are empty. When I go into Mr. Sidhu's classroom, his head is down on his desk. There are stacks of papers everywhere. I think he's asleep and wonder if I should come back at a different time. But it's 4:15. If he's sleeping, he should probably wake up so he can go home. I knock lightly on the door even though it's open. He grunts softly and looks up at me with red eyes.

"Sorry to interrupt," I say.

He looks at the clock on the wall.

"No, no. I must have nodded off for a

second. I was up all night with the baby. Come in. Sit." He gestures to the desk near his.

"Did you hear about the whole After Grad thing?" I ask, sitting down.

"Kids can be cruel, Sofie. I'm sorry they're putting you through it. Tell me you're still going to Grad."

"I don't know. I hate to admit it, but I'm scared. What if they do something horrible to me? I don't want any trouble and it doesn't seem worth it. It's just a stupid tradition anyway. Totally outdated."

"You bought tickets though, right?"

I nod.

"Then you should go. Even if you think it's outdated or silly or whatever. You can't let other people change the way you behave. Don't give them that power."

He opens his desk drawer and pulls out a KitKat, breaks it in two, and gives me the part with the wrapper.

I take a bite. "I don't know what I did to make someone hate me so much."

"With some people you don't have to do anything. And their hatred says more about them than it does about you."

When I get home, Clea's sitting at the dining room table with my mom. There's a pot of tea and two cups between them.

"What are you doing here?" I ask.

"Looking for you. I was worried."

Mom chimes in, "Me too. Where have you been all day?"

"You didn't return any of my texts," Clea says.

"I turned off my phone."

"You what?" My mom is shocked. She probably never thought she'd hear those words from me.

"I drove to the beach and sat there, staring out at the water all day. Then I went back to school. Then I came here."

"Clea tells me you're a target at school," Mom says.

"Not really. No. They're just some idiots who aren't even brave enough to say anything to my face. Just cowards."

"Cowards can be dangerous," Mom says.

"You know what's more dangerous? Giving in to them. Screw them all."

Clea gets up and puts her arms around me. In her embrace, I am tempted to shed the tears I've been holding back. Instead, I take her by the hand. I look into her eyes.

I say, "Let's go tux and dress shopping this weekend."

"We don't have to go, you know."

"Yes, we do."

That night I go through my closet and find the loudest outfit I have. I pair up some bright leopard-print tights with a dress that has a huge cat face on it, the kind of thing I'd wear in Portland, but not here. I've got some hot pink plastic hoop earrings that go with the hot pink ends in my hair. The pièce de résistance: heels. I have never worn them to school, but this is an occasion. Tomorrow I'm declaring total independence from the stupidity of the Sombies.

The next morning, I pick up Clea thirty minutes before the bell rings. When she comes to the door, I see that she's wearing one of the outfits we bought in the States. She looks amazing. It's not her clothing — she's gorgeous, don't get me wrong — it's her eyes. She's mesmerizing. Protective and fierce. I've seen her look determined, but today, she's downright intimidating. She kisses me and pulls me toward her. We're united. Nothing can go wrong. We pull into the parking lot like movie stars ready to hit the red carpet.

But then. I can't move. Can't undo my seat belt. Can't even breathe properly.

"You okay?" Clea asks.

I nod, trying to convince myself that I am. I'm not. "I'm scared."

"Don't be. They're just Sombies. They can't do anything."

"I know." But I'm not sure I do. According to the Internet, queer kids get beat up, bullied, thrown into Dumpsters and garbage cans.

Killed. I'm not ready for any of that, not even the strange looks.

"Tell me what you need," Clea says in a calm voice.

And then it hits me. "Lipstick."

I'm femme. I can do this. I unzip my backpack and pull out the red lipstick I got from the drugstore. The exact same one the girl in Portland lent me. It's so attention-grabbing, so unabashedly there. It oozes, *Yeah, I know you're looking. Go ahead.*

I apply it. Clea shakes her head at me, but she has the biggest smile I've ever seen.

"Ready," I say. She gets out of the car first and comes around to my side. I put my arm in hers and together we stroll toward the front doors as if nothing's changed since that night on the dance floor at Holocene. And it hasn't. We are who we are. And thanks to the Sombies we know who we are.

We enter the school like we own the place and even though I'm half expecting hordes of undead corpses to come at us, I'm ready for them. It's just like the video game that Paul and I used to play, except instead of a toy gun, I'm armed with confidence and the best girlfriend on the entire planet.

To my amazement, everyone looks as harmless as cows grazing on grass. Blank expressions all over. The one exception is Luanne, who's headed straight for us, her posse in tow.

"Sofie," she calls out from down the hall. "Wait up."

"Yeah?"

"It's over. You won."

"What?" I ask.

"Brooke-Lynn is Har Lee. She's the one who set up After Grad. She's been suspended. When Paul heard that she was behind it, he dumped her. Then he reported her to the principal. It's all anyone talked about yesterday."

"Seriously?"

"Yep."

I'm crying. My makeup is going to be a hideous mess. My protective mask is melting away, but I don't care. Maybe I don't need it anymore.

"Luanne." I clutch her arm, bite my lip, and fight back the tears.

"Honey, you're freakin' amazing, okay?" She's teary now too. "The whole school is going to stand by you. The GSA, everyone in Interfaith. Ditto Knitting Club. Paul. His friends."

"Really?" I'm totally crying.

Luanne nods. "We love you, Sofie. Don't even worry about that psycho what's her face."

"Clea and I decided last night that we're going to Grad no matter what."

"I'm so proud of you," Luanne says.

We both rush off to class. For me, that means Slow Science, so I have time to sit at the back and digest the new information.

I text Paul. "Is it true? Did you break up with her?"

"Yup."

"☹"

"Nah. Was sick of hearing about her hair.

Can't believe what she did to u."

I feel so relieved to be texting with Paul. I've missed being friends. Maybe we won't talk in the hallways, but it feels good just to exchange a few words. That afternoon I drift through the hallways feeling light and free.

EPILOGUE

I don't know for certain that Brooke-Lynn and her gang won't do something hurtful to me at Grad, but I decide it doesn't matter. I need to live my life the way I want. One day Brooke-Lynn will be on some reality TV show for child-actor washouts who get bad plastic surgery, and I'll make big bowls of buttery popcorn during all thirteen weeks of it and watch her suffer. Or I'll forgive her. Whichever comes first.

Clea and I go thrift-store shopping in Mission and find a dark purple velour suit that almost fits her. Mrs. Thompson has a minor meltdown when we take it back to her place. I don't know what's worse in her opinion: that it is a man's suit or that it is second-hand. But she gets over it and even forks out for a tailor. As for me, I score a mint green polka-dotted dress that is just incredible. No alterations needed. My goal now is to find some Kool-Aid to match my dress, so I can colour my hair. I'm thinking lime. And I'll bleach it first, so the green's kind of pastel-coloured. Maybe matching eyeshadow too, while I'm at it.

In English class, we write a mock Provincial exam, which means writing an entire essay in an hour. It's scary, but I do it. I write about Candy Crush as a metaphor for life. How life is a process and there's no point in rushing through whatever comes our way. What's important is enjoying the game.

Mr. Davidson gives the essay back to me a week later with a huge, circled red B+ on the top right-hand corner. Highest mark ever.

Clea gets a big envelope from the University of British Columbia offering her a scholarship to study literature. She hugs me so tightly I'm afraid my ribs will snap.

"What about Portland?" I ask.

"Too expensive. Too far away."

My own acceptance letter comes a few days later. I'll be going to Vancouver Community College to study cooking. It's perfect. The first step toward my dream life. And the coolest part? Since Kurt transferred from his California university to UBC, Clea's parents said they will rent an apartment that Clea and Kurt can share near the university, so they don't have to drive so much. And I get to stay over as often as I want. Since I have the tin can, I can drive us home on weekends and work with Mom and contribute to rent or groceries or both. One thing is for sure. We're officially out of Sombieland.

Grad night is cheesier and more awesome than I expected. Clea surprises me with a white freesia corsage. I surprise her right back with a craft I've been working on for a while, a knitted, dark purple corsage. It's super cute and pretty butch and it goes very well with her suit. We drive there in the tin can, so we can put the savings on a limo toward visiting Aunt Sarah in Portland. Before we go in, we share a Red Bull because we're crazy like that. I've got my arms around Clea and I feel glamorous in my vintage dress. We're ready to make an entrance.

Brooke-Lynn and her friends are all standing outside the hotel lobby in their black minidresses and stiletto heels. They're smoking and glowering. No one makes eye contact with me and I don't look at them as we walk past. Inside, it's dark and decorated and there's so much to look at.

Out of the corner of my eye, I see Paul with Rachel Mackenzie, his new girl. I laugh to myself. That guy wastes no time. When our eyes meet, I smile. He smiles back. We're both holding other people's hands right now and it feels good to acknowledge each other in public.

To my shock, he drops Rachel's hand and comes over to me.

"Hi," he says directly to me. Then he addresses both of us. "You two look great. It's good to see you here. I didn't know if you'd come."

"It's Grad," I say. "We wouldn't miss it."

"Wanna dance?" he asks. I'm taken aback. In my confusion, I look to Clea. She gives me an encouraging nod, so I agree.

Paul and I walk to the dance floor together and — wouldn't you just know it? — the music switches to a slow song. Paul takes the lead. I put my arms around his shoulders and relax into the comfortable position I used to love so much. He seems a lot smaller to me. Clea's taller and her shoulders are broader. I'm used to her body now, but this is nice.

"Just so you know," Paul says, "I'm sorry about everything."

"Me too." We dance in silence for a while. I realize there's something more I want to say and I may never have the chance again. After tonight I don't think we'll be seeing much of each other anymore. "Paul?"

"Yeah?"

"You were my first love and you will always be special to me."

He holds me close and although I can't see it, I can tell he's smiling. He kisses my hair as we sway in time to the beat. I rest my head against his chest one last time and everything feels good. This is how I want to remember him. The slow song ends and we part ways.

At the end of the party, Clea takes me by the hand. As we walk out of the hotel and into the balmy night, I tell her she was right.

"About what?" she asks, looking up at the stars shining down on us.

"We have everything ahead of us," I say, clutching the railing around the Pan Pacific boardwalk in Vancouver's harbour. "This is only the beginning."

"Next year is going to be incredible."

We're overlooking the water when a seal pops up its head and looks at us. We laugh and I assume it'll leave, but it doesn't. It just floats there, staring.

I prop myself up on the guardrail and swing my legs out in front. Clea puts her arms around my waist to protect me from falling.

"Don't worry," she reassures me. "I've got you."

I feel her breath on the back of my neck. There are tingles all the way down my spine as she holds me in perfect silence — the two of us and our marine friend.

"Clea?"

"Yeah?"

"I love you."

"I love you more."

MARQUIS

Québec, Canada